LIKE FATHER LIKE SON

LIKE FATHER LIKE SON

DAVID TIPPING

David Tipping

THE SUNDIAL PRESS

LIKE FATHER LIKE SON
First published by The Sundial Press 2012

THE SUNDIAL PRESS
Sundial House, The Sheeplands, Sherborne, Dorset DT9 4BS
www.sundialpress.co.uk

Copyright
© David Tipping 2012

David Tipping has asserted his moral right to be identified as the author of this work
in accordance with the Copyright, Designs and Patents Act, 1988

A CIP catalogue record for this book is available from the British Library

All rights reserved. This publication may not be reproduced,
stored in a retrieval system or transmitted in any form or
by any means, electronic, mechanical, photocopying, recording
or otherwise, without prior permission in writing from the publishers.

ISBN 978-1-908274-14-4

Printed in Great Britain by the MPG Books Group
Bodmin and King's Lynn.

Contents

FEBRUARY	1
SPRING	25
SUMMER	87
AUTUMN	137
THE FOLLOWING FEBRUARY	155

FEBRUARY

IT is midday on Sunday, in the Dorset village where Harold and Thelma Ingram have lived for the past sixteen years in contented retirement. It is the day of their annual 'At Home'. They stand just inside the lobby of the front door, which they have opened to welcome the first guests. Inside the house their son Luke is helping with the final preparations directed by his teenaged children, Leo and Margaret, who are more familiar with the domestic arrangements. Luke has just returned to England after fifteen years in Hong Kong.

Harold thinks of who will be coming. Thelma ponders the sermon she heard an hour ago given by her friend, the rector, Tom Foster. 'Thou shalt not covet thy neighbour's wife.' She smiles; had anyone ever coveted her? Tom will be coming this morning, with his wife Dorothy. Harold, who never goes to church, likes and admires them both. Then there are the Halls, Rupert and his wife Penny, of Luke's generation. They are a devoted couple, with an 'open' marriage. Rupert has come from London and Penny is recently established in the village. These two couples are the regulars, the Ingrams' close friends. Among the others is Michael Green, most kindly described as an enthusiast; and there are various old acquaintances. This year there are newcomers, the Willoughbys, whom Thelma will introduce to their neighbours.

Soon there will be the animated talk, the pouring of drinks, the frequent bursts of laughter and the bending of ears to gossip. Harold and Thelma are content for the moment to stand silent, surveying the garden where snowdrops announce the coming season. In the village all is still and quiet; the only movement is in the sky, where dark clouds have been casting a gloomy shroud. A moment later, the Fosters push back the garden gate, with Rupert and Penny close behind. It is the moment when the sun finds a clearing and the sudden light is like the drawing back of a curtain.

The party was in full swing. Leo and Margaret had crossed paths in the middle of the room, carrying their trays of canapés, crudités and other enticing niblets, for which the two 'children' were the best customers.

'Uncle Rupert is getting in touch with his feminine side,' Leo said to his sister, looking to where their old friend from London was talking to 'Grandma Thelma'.

'I think he finds that side more accessible,' Margaret replied, and was still young enough to giggle. They were enjoying the party, this annual event for their winter half-term. The room felt crowded with the twenty or more people present. Rupert Hall, standing at the window and enthusing to Thelma on the beauty of her garden, looked round at the teenagers.

'I heard that, you awful children. When you've decided which side you're going to cultivate, let me know and I may have some advice for you.'

It was said with pretended admonition; the humour in his eye suggested something softer.

'They are growing up fast,' he said.

'It is some time since I heard them call you "Uncle".'

'My honorary status is used for irony. I expect they think it post-modern. It is barely post-pubic.'

'But your avuncular attachment won't fade, I hope. Or that of Penny, though I'm not sure of the adjective. Auntly?'

'Antic, perhaps. We remain very attached, Thelma.'

'It has meant a lot to them, as you know, with not having a mother.'

'And to both of us. But talking of the grown-ups, I see my dear wife locked in earnest conversation with your son, the hero home from Hong Kong. You must be glad to have him back.'

'Yes, very. But what will he do next, I wonder? More of that another time, Rupert. I must circulate. I see earnest Michael Green looking lost.'

'Not for words, surely?'

'No, for a listener.'

Rupert wandered over to talk to a fellow guest, and Thelma moved off to her duties as hostess. She was a tall, imposing woman, forthright in speech and manner. At seventy-two, she was four years younger than Harold, and showed better health and vigour. Her hair, once auburn, was faded and partly grey, contrasting with Harold's abundant silvery thatch. Thelma inspired a deep affection in her friends, though her firm gaze and deliberate tone would sometimes induce timidity in those meeting her for the first time. She was aware of this and tried to counter it.

Michael Green, whom she now confronted, she knew to be immune to feelings of timidity or self-doubt. He was a distinctive figure. His long, unbrushed hair had once been jet black, but now was flecked with grey. His unkempt beard sported two tones of grey, a dark inner core, and a lighter outer band straggling unevenly from the edges. He had dressed in a suit, with just a T-shirt under the jacket. The looseness of fit suggested either a loss of weight since its purchase many years ago, or that he had acquired it second-hand. His most distinctive feature was a beatific smile. On his own, his smile glowed quietly like a pilot flame waiting for the larger ignition. This would happen when someone stood before him.

He was relieved at Thelma's presence. His life-partner, Jean Hardy, was engaged elsewhere with a Dr Willoughby, the newcomer. He would have liked to have Jean with him now, in her multi-coloured splendour. His previous listener, who had announced a sudden and urgent need to pass some information to another guest, had abandoned him. But he was happy now to unburden himself to his hostess; she for her part was content to listen for a few minutes.

He started without hesitation, 'Thelma, hello, did you notice how late they were with the dustbins on Monday? I called the Council on Tuesday morning to give them a talking-to. No, hang on. I tell a lie. It was Tuesday afternoon. I remember because Jean was late getting up that morning, and it was after lunch…' He continued to interrupt himself, without reaching any obvious conclusion. Thelma was waiting for a natural break to make her escape. She spent a lot of time in the village, visiting, listening, sometimes having to offer comfort, but usually finding the right moment to leave. Her companion on these exercises, the rector's wife, Dorothy, was nearby. They could swap places in a minute. In the corner of her eye, she could see some of her other guests, and felt that the party was going well. She could hear Tom, the rector, talking to Mrs Willoughby – Thelma had forgotten her first name – and she nodded at Harold as he passed, a bottle in each hand, topping up glasses with red or white wine.

Her son Luke, as Rupert had remarked, was talking to Rupert's wife, Penny. Leo and Margaret had introduced Penny to their father, on her arrival with Rupert that morning. Rupert and Luke had met in the City once or twice in the past. Penny and Luke had never met, though they knew each other well at second hand, through the children. They were now at the point of taking each other in, engaging in small talk. Luke Ingram was tall, with fair, almost flaxen hair. Not so much handsome as noticeable, his face rather older than his forty-four years, perhaps, some might say, from too many of them lived in the East. He, if it were put to him, would put it down to an excess of air-conditioning. He had inherited from his father a scholarly look, and the bent of mind that confirmed it. His voice was soft and he spoke slowly. Penny stood as high as his chin; she had an animated face and her speech tended to the staccato. There was something of the gamine about her that he thought some men might find attractive. Luke noticed her rather untidy appearance, her thin hair swinging around when she talked. He found her quite different from how he had imagined.

'It's very strange our not having met, and my knowing your children so well.'

'Yes. I have seen you and Rupert in photos, read about you in many letters, and of course I heard even more at first hand when they came out to Hong Kong for their holidays. But living abroad had many disadvantages. Losing touch with home was not the least. I'm looking forward to putting that right.'

'What persuaded you to settle in Dorset?'

'That must be a good question. I have been asked it five times since my first drink.'

'Well, if you haven't had too many, you should have perfected your answer.'

'Here comes my father with bottles. Perfection may follow.'

Harold offered wine to Penny, who declined.

'I do admire a lady who knows when to say no. Luke? Yes, I thought you might,' and he filled the proffered glass. 'Penny, you'll have to teach him moderation.' With this, Harold moved off to refill the glass he had left for himself on the mantelpiece.

'Your question: I have not exactly settled here. I arrived two or three weeks ago, and I've been trying to get sorted out. I'm renting a little cottage for six months, where I can be near the old folk, and my young ones at school. The idea is to be quiet and to think what I want to do.'

'You think you may be rather young for the rural life?'

'I am too young not to be gainfully employed: you are quite right. But I was fortunate in my last employment; I now have the opportunity to think of a better way to spend my life than making money for employers and shareholders. But I can ask you the same question. You've also moved here recently, I'm told.'

'Yes. And I've not been here much longer than you. Rupert and I have always lived in London. He can't escape. I mean he's economically and emotionally tied to the place. I was, but it became weaker for me, and finally I felt I had to get out. So we compromised. We bought *Coralita* last summer, in the village here, for me to run as a Bed and Breakfast. My very own little business, something I've always wanted. Rupert divides his time between here and London, though it's a very unequal division. We sold the London house, and got a flat for Rupert. I go up when the spirit moves me, and business permitting. But the spirit seldom moves, and I've found myself increasingly busy. Frankly, I love having something of my own to build up and try to be good at. You'd be surprised at how much there is to running a B and B.'

They were interrupted by Dorothy Foster. She was one of those women so obviously kind and good-natured that people naturally smiled when they faced her.

'Luke, it seems such a long time. I was so glad to hear you've given up foreign parts. Tom and I were hoping to see you in church this morning. No slacking, now.'

'It must indeed be a long time, Dorothy, or you might have remembered I am not a believer.'

'Tut! That is no reason for absence. I must get Tom on to you.'

'Not literally, I hope.'

'Luke, I am the only one allowed to make jokes about Tom's …' – she hesitated – 'build.' But she laughed. She enjoyed little jokes about her husband's rotundity, though she preferred to be the source of them.

At some point, guests began to go. They dispersed into or around the village, some on foot, some by car. It was towards the end of the twentieth century, and Lynchets Wood was quieter than most parts of England.

In the house there remained the customary core of family and friends, standing in a loose semi-circle round the fireplace. There were the five members of the three generations of Ingrams: Harold and Thelma, Luke, and Leo and Margaret. And there were the four friends: Tom and Dorothy, Rupert and Penny. A fire had been lit that morning, and glowed decoratively behind the glass doors of the stove.

'Tom,' Dorothy addressed her husband. 'I have told Luke I would put you on to him. Slackness in church-going: it won't do. He seems to think agnosticism an excuse for absence.'

'I am surrounded in my Parish by heathens, pagans, atheists and agnostics. There is even a touch of New Age, Travelling, and animist greenery. But I am never discouraged. They will all be gathered in, in God's good time.' There was a touch of rotundity in his speech, nicely matching his figure. He radiated good humour and imperturbability.

'The gathering in would be at the Last Harvest Festival, then,' said Leo.

'Leo has learnt how to enunciate the capital letters,' Margaret added.

'Michael is one of the green, eponymously and ideologically,' observed Rupert, ignoring the children, 'and certainly animated, but improbably animist. Simply verbose and verbosely simple.'

'Michael Green is impossible,' Harold said. 'No one who inflicts such deadly boredom on people has the right to look so absurdly happy. He looks like the Second Coming, and talks like a local authority newsletter.'

'I am obliged to take a more charitable view,' said the rector. 'Happiness is a special gift, and we shouldn't question it. One of the ways it is earned is from doing good works, and Michael does those in plenty. But I am bound to say, he is not quite how I imagine the Second Coming. And I hope I shall be given prior warning of such an event. Actually,' the rector said, rotating his mass in the direction of Rupert, 'despite his support for animal rights, I believe Michael sees himself as agnostic rather than animist.'

Harold snorted. 'Agnosticism is not a tenable position,' he said. 'The expression of doubt implies the existence of something to doubt. I am not even sure I accept atheism, for a similar reason. The farthest I might go is to believe in a God who would happily accept that I need not believe in him.'

'That is trying to have the best of both worlds, this one and the next,' said Thelma.

'I have no idea about the best or the worst in the next world,' said Harold, 'it is enough having to avoid the worst in this one.'

'We are fortunate in receiving this Sunday lesson in theology,' said Leo to Margaret.

'Would Grandpa allow the existence of theology without God?' asked Margaret.

'Grandpa does not allow the existence of empty glasses while there is wine in the bottle. Now, what about a last fill-up, everyone?' Harold asked. With no takers other than Luke, he filled his own glass to keep his son company.

Thelma turned to her husband. 'Harold, you and Luke should set a better example to the young ones. Everywhere you look, there seem to be bad examples. Just last week, drunken teenagers set a car alight in St Giles.'

'I deplore such behaviour,' Harold said, 'it gives drunkenness a bad name.'

Before Thelma could reply, Dorothy said, 'Harold, perhaps a little less secular wine and more of the Communion variety would be better for the two of you.'

Tom chuckled. 'I leave evangelism to my wife. She is better at it than I am.'

'She is better at it than I am,' said Thelma. 'I had to abandon from the very beginning any hope of saving my husband's soul. And after forty-five years of marriage I am still wondering if he has one.'

'A Christian and an atheist, living in such marital harmony, is a refreshing sight. It is good to be reminded of the one elemental force conquering all others, that lies behind the attraction of opposites,' said Rupert.

'Harrumph!' from Harold, who then added, 'Opposites nonsense. There is only one opposite that matters in the choice of a mate: sex. May I remind you, those whom the gods would couple they first make mad. And blind. The poets may do with it what they will. And for those afflicted it is the only time in life that they are likely to attain the state of poetry. But that period of passion and insanity make an inescapable ritual played out for the preservation of the human race. What woman in her right mind would sensibly choose to spend her life with a man who cannot graciously accept finding his newspaper every morning crumpled up all over the house? Without the biological necessity of blind desire there could have been no Luke Ingram to perpetuate the family name.'

'Blind desire, indeed! I merely made the mistake of feeling sorry for you.'

'Bravo, Thelma,' from Dorothy. 'I should like to hear Harold tell us what he thinks no man in his right mind would sensibly take on in a mate.'

'Chivalry seals my lips.'

'Chivalry is not making a very good job of it,' retorted Thelma.

'A good marriage can withstand most obstacles,' said Tom, 'even the daily dismemberment of one's newspaper. One of the greatest problems for a couple, other than one of them running off with someone else, is the crashing of a skeleton from a cupboard. I have seen that more than once. It can need the re-writing of years of mutual history.'

'Harold can be grateful that his problem is of such minor, mundane character. And I suppose I should be grateful that we have come all these years with no skeletons crashing out of cupboards,' Thelma said, raising an eyebrow at her husband. He gave her a cheery little wave, barely conscious of the faint, uneasy stirring that most men would experience on these occasions.

The Fosters and the Halls left soon after. Harold put his arm round Thelma's unslim waist, and told her it had been a good party.

A kiss on the cheek said more. The family now prepared itself for a light meal before clearing the debris. They sat round the kitchen table.

'How did you get on with Penny?' his mother asked Luke.

'I liked her; she is thoughtful and animated.' He paused before adding, 'And mated in an interesting manner. Rupert is splendid, but odd for a husband.'

'They are a devoted and happy couple,' she said. 'He is certainly a feminine man, and I've heard of boyfriends. She is a feminine woman, and – or should it be 'but'? – I have heard doubts as to which way she is most inclined. I don't know about that, and it does no good to gossip. I've told you, her mother and I were close friends at Cambridge. That's the connection. Penny used to visit us here. That's why she grabbed *Coralita* when it came on the market. Not to escape Rupert, though some might say that, but to escape London. She's always been an independent one. But they have been married for getting on fifteen years, and that says enough. They give each other freedom, as many people do these days. For them it seems to work.'

'I like Rupert,' Harold added. 'He says what he likes. An earnest female once asked him if he was gay. I was there. He replied that he was sometimes gay, often gloomy, but usually homosexual.' Harold laughed. 'I like that "usually".'

'Luke, I think your children are receiving instruction in more than theology, today.'

'Don't worry about us, Grandma,' Margaret said. 'We cannot be shocked. We have to be careful not to shock the older generation.'

'I'm afraid that's right, Ma.'

Rupert Hall was a slight, mercurial-looking man, quick of tongue and light on his feet. It was easy to imagine him dancing. He had dark, loose hair, and black eyes that often flashed with glee, and could snap cold with anger or melancholy. Many women had fallen for him; only Penny had won his heart. Many men had fallen for him; a few had won, but never for long. His voice was high tenor, and at times sounded poised on the edge of song.

He was somewhat of a mystery, even to those who knew him well. This was despite, or perhaps because of, his apparent openness. He had 'come out' some years ago, and told his friends he enjoyed the experience so much that he had repeated it, like a debutante extending her season. In fact he was careful, sensitive to the occasions and the company in which this might embarrass people.

He knew that people wondered about his marriage. He wondered about it too. He was not like those gay men who had married so as to appear to the world – and to themselves – as 'normal'. He did not see that as applying to him. He had undertaken marriage, not to acquire a shield of respectability, but because he had found a woman he loved and wanted always to be there. He and Penny were kindred spirits; she had told him from the beginning that she liked women as well as men; they had recognised and respected the truth about each other. They liked to say that it was a case of ambiguity at first sight. Even so, he often felt surprised at how successful their union had been.

Not least of the mysteries about Rupert was how he earned his daily bread, and managed such copious helpings of jam to spread on it. It was not that his consumption was conspicuous in any vulgar sort of way, but there were hints of large investments and of frequent, comfortable travel. Their house in London appeared modest; it was in a street where a modest terrace house might have bought a castle in Scotland. Rupert had owned one of those too, as an investment, and had sold it well. His profession as freelance financial journalist gave him contacts for stories, tips and opportunities for investment, about which he was mostly silent. He was silent on his deals, even to Penny. She recognised this as a part of his life that he preferred to keep to himself. He did not want to 'bother her with the boring details of his daily grind'. It only bothered her when she thought he looked anxious, but she seldom pressed him to talk about it. One of the secrets of success in their marriage, as they both knew, was the discretion they accorded each other.

It was the morning after Thelma's party: Rupert and Penny were sitting at breakfast, intermittently talking and reading their newspapers.

'I crashed out fairly quickly last night,' Rupert said, 'I've been having a busy time, and more to come. But tell me, what did you make of our friend Luke?'

'He's not as I imagined him. Not obviously the wheeler-dealer trader type. He seems quite bookish.'

'I know someone in the City who came across him in Hong Kong. He said Luke was known by some as "the monk", perhaps because he kept off cocaine and only got drunk once a week. See how modestly he lives here. His car is second-hand, and unglamorous. He doesn't wear the expensive designer brands, and he is not an obvious high-spender. He is almost as modest as I am. But he had a reputation as a very shrewd dealer. He would have put away a tidy sum, several seven figures, I imagine. But more to the point, he's good-looking. I always go for that tall, languid look. And the flaxen hair. I wonder that he's stayed single all these years. Do we know anything about his love life?'

'It's not the first thing I thought of asking him, and Thelma has said nothing. We shall have to wait and see whether anything turns up.'

'Or anyone. But there is something strange about a successful man suddenly giving it all up, and coming to rusticate for six months. It's strange enough for someone like you to exchange the London buzz for a Dorset village, but at least you have a purpose here.'

'Yes, it's odd. I, as you say, have a purpose here. I love it. You know that, don't you? This combination of home and business just suits me perfectly. I'm so looking forward to the summer, my first season, when things should get into full swing.'

'I'm glad for you. But we do see less of each other now, don't we? And I'm sorry I can't spend more time here. I can't see myself doing a Luke just yet. Or ever, come to that.' Rupert shuffled his paper, hesitated, put it down and turned to his wife.

'Penny, Poppet, we were talking about the possibility of an extension here, for those two extra bedrooms. Well, I think we'll have to put that on hold, just for now. I'm getting very tied up at the moment. Time and money, as they say. I'm having to catch up with both of them.'

'Rupert, we're not in trouble are we?'

'Good heavens, no. But we should, for the rest of this year, proceed with just a little restraint. Anyway, you're going to be far too busy getting the business started to want to have to bother with expanding it just yet. Think of all the palaver you've been through just to get the place sorted out this far.'

'The business should start to bring in some money this year.'

'Of course. And now I have to get that train. I'll call you later about next weekend. I may have to go up to Scotland again.'

'Oh, Rupert! Do try to come down. I need you to look after me.'

Rupert guffawed. 'You need me to keep you on the straight and narrow. I'll do my best, little Penny.'

Sitting in the train, on the way to Waterloo, Rupert wondered whether Penny was heading for an affair with Luke. Penny was not promiscuous, he knew that, but from time to time someone interesting, attractive, suitable, came along, and she would be flung into something she could not always control. He hoped she would be all right, this time, should anything happen. He thought he sensed some chemistry between them, observing them at the Ingrams yesterday; but Penny had shown no sign of any special feeling for the man, at breakfast. His mind switched to his own affairs, or rather what might be becoming an affair with Paul. They had met in a City pub eleven days ago, and discovered a mutual interest in Scotland, loving the geography, liking the property market, and seeming to like each other. Rupert had been thinking about him all through breakfast, while listening to Penny.

That morning, after breakfast, Harold Ingram stepped out from his house into the lane that led to the main village street of Lynchets Wood. He enjoyed this moment in the day. Having completed the domestic duties that, over the years, he had assigned to himself for each morning, he left Thelma in the house with the rather more numerous duties remaining for her. His job now was to walk to the village shop to purchase the daily newspaper, together with whatever

Thelma had written on the back of the envelope which he clutched in his hand, hoping not to forget it was there.

The steep hillside came down to the edge of the village. The lynchets were in sharp relief in the pale February sun. These narrow, ancient terraces, covered by a skin of grass, tight as on a ribcage, often made him wonder at the tenacity of the ancient farmers who must once have cultivated the steep slopes. There were no signs of any wood that might have given the village the second half of its name. Village historians – and Harold was a leading figure – argued that the trees had been cut down to make the space and provide the wood for the original dwellings. There was nowhere else, with the hill on one side, and the flood plain of the River Pant on the other, where the settlement could have started.

He walked with a slight limp. His doctor had told him it might be the result of a war wound, affecting him now with the onset of arthritis. At seventy-six, he felt healthy enough, and the occasional pain in his leg was a good reason for spending more time in his chair, reading. He was a tall, gaunt man, with a Roman nose and a craggy face. He had been likened to a long dead English character actor, with the addition of a massive crop of silvery hair.

He had had an active life. After war service in the Navy, he had returned to Oxford to complete his degree in history. With a good First behind him, he had been pointed by his tutor to the diplomatic service, and that is where he had passed the next thirty or so years. He had not achieved the highest rank or grandest postings, but had happily filled senior posts in various small, mostly undemanding countries. His second name being Edgar, he liked to explain that his final promotion was due to his initials. Modesty was not in his nature, but sometimes had a diplomatic use.

He had seen the world, and met many people. He had felt the wheels of power, around him and above him. Occasionally his hand was on a lever. But towards the end he was becoming disenchanted with the encroachments of his various masters, some of whom he found it difficult to respect. He was glad to take his retirement at sixty. His pension and his savings, helped by a small legacy from his parents, had enabled him to buy Broad Oaks, which he and Thelma had enjoyed for these past sixteen years. Their material aspirations were modest enough and their means were sufficient: for holidays and the purchase of occasional luxuries from one or two carefully chosen shops in London. Most of their needs were met from the nearby town of St Giles, which is where he was going this morning, taking Luke with him.

Half an hour later, driving Luke into town, he said to his son, 'I suppose it's too early to ask how your plans are going?'

'It is, rather. I'm not rushing it, you know. I'm here till August. But coming back to England after so many years abroad is like a major internal refurbishment. You have to give the dust time to settle.'

'I can see that. Your mother and I love having you so near, but we don't expect you to make it permanent. I mean, you wouldn't see us as a doddery old couple to keep an eye on, would you?'

Luke laughed. 'I sometimes see myself as a doddery young son you feel you have to keep an eye on.'

'Well, that's all right, then. Mutual misunderstanding has always been a good basis for a happy family.' Harold chuckled.

'I am trying to sort out my thoughts. I am writing it down, what I've been doing these past fifteen years. It's been a fascinating mixture of economics, politics, social customs, people and high finance. Low finance, come to that. It occupied me completely while it lasted, and then it went a bit sour. Having it written down will give it perspective; then I can put it behind me. Move on, as they say.'

'Good luck to you. I once thought of doing something like that. I think inertia killed the idea, along with the Official Secrets Act. And I have always been suspicious of public servants who go on to blab and blubber about themselves in print. But it's different in a case like yours. Ah! Here we are.'

They went their separate ways, Harold to his bank, Luke to the bookshop. Later, he would collect his car from its MOT and make his own way home. In the bookshop he browsed quite happily for ten or fifteen minutes, and not finding the book he wanted, he ordered it and wandered down the main street with time on his hands. A coffee aroma from an open door held him, and he saw Penny about to enter.

'So it's coffee time. May I join you?'

'Why, Luke! By all means.'

They found a small table at the back of the crowded coffee shop.

He got his question in first. 'How's the B and B business doing? We didn't get very far with that yesterday.'

'Well, I opened in November, after a summer of builders, plumbers and electricians laying siege to my life. It's been a quiet winter season for me, but I now appear in one or two of the guides, and I've had a few visitors. Bookings are looking up. Word of mouth is always best, though, so if you have friends asking for the best possible bed and breakfast in these parts, you'll know where to send them.'

He watched her speaking. She was quite a small woman, perhaps three or four years younger than him; she spoke rapidly with an animated expression. Her head nodded, her untidy hair swung about, and her eyes shone. His own speech, by contrast, he heard as slow and deliberate. And, watching Penny, he realised that he normally kept his head still when he was talking.

'Well, it's quite likely I shall. The place I'm renting is fine for the children, but I wouldn't want to squeeze adults in. I know the children are virtually adult, but you know what I mean.'

'We didn't get very far with the story of your life at Thelma's yesterday. No one ever gave me a coherent account of what you were doing in Hong Kong, apart from making pots of money. Wasn't that worth staying at? I didn't go into my little business expecting to make a fortune, but it seems to be taken as a measure of success.'

'That's very true. But I came to find that success at making money was less and less satisfying. You will enjoy seeing the happy faces of your guests. I just saw columns of figures. What I did was strenuous and demanding, in time and mental effort. It left little over. I was lucky with a formula or two that I had, working in derivatives. It gave me enough to get out. Any longer and the whole thing might have blown. Now I'm glad to be out of it.'

'But you enjoyed it once?'

'Oh, yes. Technically it can be very stimulating, like playing a good hand at bridge. Some people do it because they like to see the stuff piling up. Also there's the satisfaction of pitting your wits against the system, the markets. In the end, though, it gets in the way of other ideas, other ways of thinking. Look, I prefer asking questions to answering them.'

'But you've hardly said anything! What did you do when you were not making your piles of money?'

'You should know about money men. You're married to one. A financial journalist like Rupert lives at least on the fringes of that unnatural world; he is certainly familiar with the type; and not unsuccessful himself, as I've heard. The children used to tell me how the two of you went off on exotic holidays, living it up in tax havens.'

He thought Penny looked disconcerted.

'Those trips were business,' she said, 'with a short holiday tacked on. It was the only way I could get him to have one.'

'Past tense?'

'We are getting away from you, Luke Ingram. I was asking you how you relax when you're not making money.'

'People have an image of traders as mindlessly splashing out on everything extravagant. Some are inclined that way, and if your shopping time is limited, you tend to spend with more intensity. I have never been that way inclined. I really do prefer a good book to a noisy restaurant that overcharges, or driving a big, flashy car that can only crawl along overcrowded roads.'

'And what is your idea of a good book.'

'Oh, I'll settle for Henry James. I can honestly say he has saved me a fortune in money unspent.'

'I'm glad to hear it. I 'did' Henry James at Keele. And may he forgive me the slang.' She looked at her watch. 'I ought to be going; we must talk more another time. And remember, I want to hear the details of life as a Hong Kong money man. I am a very inquisitive woman.'

'I'll have to remember. First my father, now you. He was probing me this morning. He drove me in. I think he's a bit worried about my finding something to do. He worked until his proper retirement age. That's the norm for most people. I shall not have a retirement age unless I work for someone else, and that's what I have just escaped. We shall see. But now it's my pleasure as a money man to treat you to this coffee.'

He paid, and they left on their respective ways.

SPRING

Luke had looked up from his gardening and seen Penny cycling past.

'It's going to rain. Come and have some tea.'

Now they were seated by the window, the tea tray between them. The rain had started.

'What a dismal day,' she said.

'It is a lovely day, March at its best. Rain is falling, softly, on grass. Listen, it makes a hushing sound. Here in Dorset we get a very special, very English rain. In Cornwall they have the rude, intemperate Atlantic, bending the trees. It rushes into Devon like a giant car wash for all the log-jammed traffic. It crosses the damp flats of Somerset, and then Wiltshire welcomes it. But the deviation into Dorset is modest and genteel. It is a very polite rain, pouring as tea should be poured, in the best society, gently.'

'What is the best society?'

'Just you and me.'

'Will you pour me some more, then?'

He did so.

He noticed that today there was a quieter look about her. She was leaning back in her chair, not so actively bobbing about and nodding her head when she spoke. He hoped this was a sign of her being at ease. He felt totally so, himself, sprawling in his chair with his long legs stretched out in front of him.

'It must have been terrible when your wife died.'

He stiffened a little, and looked out of the window. A blackbird was in the birdbath, washing in the rain. It seemed unnecessary.

'We had been married just five years. Leo was four and Margaret not quite three. I came home from work that day, walked into the sitting room, and found the children standing by her chair. They knew something had happened; they were not sure what. Claire must have died just a moment before.'

The blackbird gave a shake and flew off. He watched it. Penny was silent.

'I won't try to tell you how it was over the next few weeks. I got help. My mother was marvellous. The children came down here. I came and went. When my firm offered me the job in Hong Kong I had to take it. The children would be provided for, their fares to Hong Kong paid twice a year, and I had an annual trip home. Margaret and Leo learnt to shoulder the burden of looking after their fractured father. They have done it ever since, with a fine grace.'

On that he brought his eyes back into the room, and smiled at her. 'And you came on the scene for them, quite early on.'

'Yes. Thelma rang me one day. Invited me down. I quite fell for them. Rupert and I had agreed from the beginning that we didn't want children. But here were two lovely children we could have for part-time adoption. It satisfied what little maternal instinct I ever had, without all the traumas of motherhood. As for Rupert's instincts, they are strictly avuncular. Paternity would appal him.'

'What are Chinese women like?'

'They are charming. They have midnight blue hair with a silky sheen, and neat little bosoms and bottoms. They are very polite.'

'You must have had one or two relationships in all those years – diversions from the tedium of making money? I hope I'm not being too personal.'

'You could hardly be more so, but never mind. And I prefer the word 'affair'. But yes. At first I felt it was testing my loyalty. But time passes, and when I saw so many of my friends' marriages breaking up, I had to wonder how well mine might have survived. Men seem to have an untameable element in their constitution. I don't know about women: they are more domesticated. They make nests. Their mate shields them from predators, when he is not roaming and being the predator himself. There is of course the vamp, who would seem to disprove my theory. It is a general theory and must admit exceptions.'

'You have lived too long in Hong Kong, with all those polite Chinese. You are out of date. In fact you are very old-fashioned.'

'I shall take that as a compliment.'

'Which proves my point. Tell me, do you miss any of your – oh dear! Can I think of the right word for you? I don't suppose you like the word "partner"? – your now far-distant girlfriends?'

Luke managed a dry laugh. 'Don't let's get hung up on words. "Mistress" will do nicely. Of course, being obsessed with making money, I couldn't afford to spend much time with diversions. Life in the fast lane, you know. You make do with short pit stops, then get back in the traffic without wasting too much time. I always made a point of agreeing that no affair should last more than two weeks. You can't be interested in all this.'

'I am fascinated to hear a man being so frank about the nature of masculinity. Did you never want to break the two-week rule?'

'I am being interrogated. Kundera had something to say about that.' He stopped and fidgeted. 'Something or other,' he went on. 'All these questions are giving me a blank cheque to demand a reciprocal right with you.'

'I shall be no less forthcoming than you have been. You may

bring your blank cheque with you when you come to have tea with me, and see what it will get you. Or do you prefer morning coffee? What about next Tuesday morning?'

'I can't do Tuesday mornings. I've joined a tennis club, and that's when we have our weekly mix-in. They are hardy folk. They play right through the winter – outdoors, of course.'

'I have not seen you as a tennis player.'

He spent a moment thinking of how she might have seen him. The difference could be in the exposure of his knees. He put his hands on them.

'Do not think Wimbledon,' he said, 'think geriatrics. Most of the members are retired; many are elderly, though they tend to be less doddery on the court than off. There are two old gentlemen there; I imagine they are almost my father's age, who enjoy playing singles. They run around a lot, but suffer lapses of memory over the score. Every now and then they have to come to the net, to ask each other which of them is serving. I don't have to feel embarrassed by my level of play, even though I have not played for years. And being so young, a mere forty-something stripling, I get indulged by the ladies. I have to be careful not to appear to enjoy it, in case it makes the old gentlemen jealous.'

'I am getting a picture of something that is more than tennis.'

'That seems to be what tennis is.'

'How should I picture the club?'

'I could drive you there, it is not far: a tiny place called Fontis Parva. As you might expect, it is close to Fontis Magna. It is quintessential Dorset. You drive down narrow lanes, more likely to meet a horse and rider than another car. You see hills and hummocks, fields and folds, great houses lost in big gardens, and small cottages with views to a far horizon. It is all very peaceful. I can't tell you how much I love it, after all those years in that teeming, dense, Chinese city, with its buildings, people and traffic. And then there's the club. There is a single court, carved out of the field that surrounds it. Last week the sheep were all around, ignoring our play. The lady lambs have to lie down in March, they are all pregnant, carrying the great weight of our future Sunday dinners.'

'Is that what you mean by quintessential?'

'Yes: the refinement to the fifth degree, the sublime addition to the four mundane elements that our scholastic forefathers counted. But just think: had they counted a fifth element, say metal, the sublime extra would have been the sexessence.'

'And so they stuck at four.'

'If "sex" had bothered them, they could have gone for "hex".'

'I don't think hexessence would be an improvement.'

'No. But I have diverted you from your invitation. May I come to tea tomorrow week?'

It was agreed.

Three days later Luke was walking through the village. There had been heavy rain earlier that morning, and water was running down the gutters. He thought that this might be more like standard rain, whether for Dorset or elsewhere. What rubbish he had talked to Penny; and she didn't seem to mind. It was nice that she could respond to it. He was walking on, thinking of her, when there occurred one of those coincidences normally confined to fiction. A car pulled up alongside, and there was the object of his thoughts, calling from the window.

'Can I give you a lift anywhere?'

'Anywhere?'

'I am going into St Giles. I shall be there for half an hour.'

'Perfect,' he said, and jumped in. 'I have a book to collect. I must tell you, I have been re-reading *The Ambassadors*. Maria Gostrey makes me think of you in the part.'

'Me!' she screeched. 'You surely realise that she is just a narrative device. Is that how you see me? She is there to explain to Strether the social milieu he's entering in Paris. It's so that Strether can have the story in his head.'

'Oh! And I have been disappointed that no romantic attachment develops between them.'

They passed the journey happily talking of 'H. J.', as of a mutual friend. Penny parked the car on the outskirts of town, and they entered along the tree-lined avenue leading to the main street.

'Look!' Penny exclaimed. 'I was here just the other day, and these trees had no more than bare buds. Now they are in full fling.'

'They have seen you coming, and have burst into leaf through sheer joy.'

She stopped, which made him do likewise. He turned to look at her. She stared at him, her head slightly back. She had a look of surprise, and a slight, doubtful smile. 'Do you always talk to women like this?'

'Never! But today I am like the trees. Spring is early and the sap is rising. I too am bursting into leaf.' He said this almost deadpan, with a smile even smaller than hers.

'You are a wicked man.'

'I try hard to be so.'

She put her hand under his arm, and they walked on. 'I shall have to keep a sisterly eye on you, that's for sure.'

'I have always wanted a sister.'

Reaching the end of the avenue, and before turning into the busy shopping street, she took her hand from his arm, after giving it a gentle squeeze.

Thelma and Dorothy arrived simultaneously at the door of the terraced cottage where Jean Hardy shared her life and her opinions with Michael Green. They smiled conspiratorially, while Dorothy waggled the rope of the ship's bell that hung beside the door.

'It is we outside, including half the village, who hear that thing more clearly than those inside.' Thelma said.

'But it is the recycling of resources that one must notice and applaud,' Dorothy replied.

Thelma liked her friend's sense of humour; there was always an underlying sympathy, even when she was laughing at someone. She was a slight woman, especially seen alongside Thelma's rather formidable figure; and even more so when beside her husband Tom. As the rector's wife, there were many calls on her time and kindness. Thelma knew the extent of the latter quality, and sometimes wondered whether her friend was strong enough to limit its exploitation.

The door opened and Jean welcomed them. The three of them constituted the small working-group whose job it was to prepare arrangements for the Summer Solstice Supper Party. It was an annual event held in the Village Hall on the Saturday nearest to the twenty-first of June. It had started in the nineteen-sixties, and proved so popular it had become a regular feature of village life. In the following decade, when Third World issues had come to the fore, the Supper had added a fund-raising function for global poverty. That too had remained. The present routine for planning the event had been decreed by the Parish Council, after Michael Green's election as councillor. Three ladies of the village would gather in mid-March to confer, with a target date of mid-April, to put their proposals to the Supper Committee, a sub-committee of the Parish Council, and chaired this year by Michael himself. The organisation of all these meetings, the deliberations and the lengthy process of coming to decisions, was a source of time-consuming satisfaction to all those involved.

This morning, the annual cycle was being renewed. The 'troika', or three 'lady sherpas', as Harold the ex-diplomat called them, seated themselves in Jean's kitchen, around the well-scrubbed wooden table where she and Michael took all their meals. Jean was generally regarded as the perfect partner for her eccentric-looking mate. He was seen as the lucky one. She was a generous-bosomed, generous-hearted woman who retained, in appearance and behaviour, some of the attributes of the bohemianism that had so attracted Michael as a young man. In her dress she favoured long skirts, kaftans and cloaks. Her colours were mixed, but with strong hints of Mother Earth. A few years younger than Michael's sixty years, she had changed more than he had during their life of unmarried harmony. While publicly adopting a style of feminism that mocked the bourgeois virtues of good housekeeping, privately she looked back in some dismay at the domestic squalor that she had happily embraced as a young woman. What she had held on to, she told herself, was the belief that there were more important things in life, higher values in fact, than middle-class obsessions and trivialities. What had changed, for her, was simply the recognition of hygiene as a worthy if boring necessity. The three women sat now in an immaculately clean kitchen.

'Should we elect a Chair?' she asked of the other two. 'If so, it should not be me. I'm doing the coffee.'

'Quite right, dear,' said Dorothy. 'Also it might look rather incestuous, your reporting to Michael who's now Chair of the sub-committee.'

'We don't need a Chair,' said Thelma, 'let's just talk and get on with it.'

'You're both new this year,' said Dorothy. 'I speak with the vast experience of having been on last year's group. We have to agree who is to write it all down.'

'I know,' said Thelma, 'you write it all down, Dorothy, you're good at that sort of thing. Jean will look after our refreshments, bless her, and that leaves me in the chair, to cheer you both along.'

'Well,' said Jean, 'if you're in the chair, you have to organise the thinking.'

'Quite right, Jean,' Thelma said, and turning to Dorothy she said, 'Make a note of that, Dorothy.'

Their levity continued while they settled into enjoying the coffee and homemade biscuits that Jean brought to the table. When that had been consumed and cleared away, they got down to the business of the day. They concluded with a set of six draft proposals, to be reconsidered and put in final form at their next meeting.

Luke arrived at *Coralita* on the dot of half-past three, and found Penny in the garden.

'I'm sorry to be so punctual. I mistimed it.'

'I was ready, in case.'

'Your garden is looking lovely: daffodils, and already signs of tulips. March is so fecund. I feel I have missed out on gardens, living in Hong Kong. I find myself now quite bowled over by botany. It is the science to study and admire. Where does all this stuff come from, pushing up from the ground, bursting into leaf and life? It is an annual miracle.'

'It will be a miracle if I can find the time to keep it weeded.'

He looked at the warm-coloured stone of the house, and asked, 'This is obviously not coral, or even limestone. What's the connection?'

'The previous owner had lived in the Caribbean. The name meant something to him. I like it, it suggests a mermaid of the corals.'

'Queen of the tax havens, more like. Right then, Mrs Hall, I would like you to imagine that I am an important travel agent who could send a lot of business your way. How are you going to sell me whatever it is you offer your visitors?'

She took him inside, starting downstairs. He saw the sitting room and dining room used by guests, and the kitchen that doubled as sitting room for Penny, and Rupert if he was there, when there were visitors. A small staircase at the back led to her private accommodation in a separate wing at the top.

'It is a perfect house for its purpose. We can be comfortably separate from our guests, when we have them, or use the house as we like when we haven't. And upstairs our guests have a choice of three double bedrooms, which I shall now show you.'

She led him upstairs. He had been getting physically uneasy since arriving at *Coralita*, too much aware of Penny's presence. It had been difficult to make light replies to her professional account of the B and B business. They stopped now outside an open door.

'I call this the Orange Room. I had great fun furnishing this one.'

He saw a double bed with a russet-coloured bedspread. Sun fell on it from the window. It had a soft, well-rounded look. The room seemed to offer another world, quiet, harmonious, comfortable and inviting; yet not permitted. As they stood, both looking in but now silent, their hands touched. A fierce hammering filled his head. He grabbed her and kissed her. He groaned more than spoke, telling her he wanted her. She led him into the room. Some instinct made him kick the door shut behind them on the empty house. They struggled to undress before throwing back the bedclothes and preparing themselves for love.

Later, partially uncoupled, they lay at rest.
  'I have not been a very good sister.'
  'Does it feel like incest?'
  'It does rather.'
  'Look, the sun has moved. It is off the bed.'
  'It will be back tomorrow. At the same time.'
  'Should I come again?'
  She giggled. 'That's up to you.'
  They re-engaged. This time it was slow. They made love indulgently, luxuriantly, carefully, exquisitely, lingeringly and lovingly. They then lay again, quiet and languid.
  She asked him, 'Why is sex the Latin for six?'
  'It seemed a good idea at the time. And remember, mediaeval schoolmen slept six to a bed, that's to say three monks and three nuns. It kept them warm in winter.'
  'Was that sexessential?'
  'Absolutely vital. But just think: they might have called it 'hexual intercourse'. Just as well they didn't. Those of poor aspiration would have found it difficult.'

'How so?'

'Imagine trying to say 'exual hintercourse.'

'It sounds uncomfortable.'

'Penny, I don't ever want to imagine anyone else in the world doing what we've just done.'

'That sounds far too serious. It is what people do. I have. You have. And we shall do it again, with other people. But don't let's think about that now. Just remember the two-week rule. I assume that applies to us?'

'It ought to.'

'Have you remembered what Kundera said?'

'I had not forgotten. You were asking me all those questions and I thought of one of his characters – or was it himself? – talking of interrogation as an aspect of love. Last week that word would have been out of bounds.'

'It is still out of bounds.'

'I expect you're right,' he was speaking more slowly than ever, 'love may be made but not spoken. And I must remember, with Kundera, that the analogy is with the actions of the police. I shall have to think of you as a policewoman. You would be good at it. I see you enforcing the bounds, monitoring my speech, planting a bug in my mind, putting up a camera to check my speed. It is strange for me, having to adjust to life in a country lane, after living so long in the fast one.'

Luke was stretched out, looking up at her. She was sitting up on her knees, looking down at him.

'Fast and loose. That is what you are. You mustn't play fast and loose with me, Luke.'

He was quiet for a moment, then put out his tongue at her.

'Beast!' she shouted, 'I hate you! I hate you!' She fell on him, pummelling his chest, reducing him to helpless laughter. 'I hate you, too, darling Penny, you gorgeous awful little pennyworth. I hate you, too. And I love you, I love you.' He was still laughing.

'Luke, Luke, love me, Luke.'

'Love, laugh, alliterate.'

'You talked an awful lot of rubbish, then, Luke.'

'I'm afraid it is what one does. The words just come out. It is like a parallel ejaculation. You remember what my father was saying the other day? He was joking, but the meaning was there. We are programmed to behave to each other in a certain way. It is what preserves the human race.'

'I am not in the business of preserving it, and certainly not of adding to it.'

'But think of the heavy weight of history. The making of immemorial love is what connects us to our ancestors, when men grunted in caves. And they were continuing the copulatory act of the primates they had descended from. What man added was language, consciousness and memory, the great trinity that makes us human. Then poetry was possible, and the language of love.'

'A history of the world in – was that four? – sentences. Tennyson's elms are in there somewhere. The doves are moaning and innumerable bees are murmuring. The birds and bees, in short. You can't get away from it.'

'No escape is possible. Or necessary. Or desirable.'

'So we have to surrender?'

'Only accept.'

'Will you tell Rupert?'

'Nothing will be said. Nothing will be asked. But Rupert will know. There are Chinese walls in marriage, but the membrane is thin. Truth seeps through by osmosis. The essential truth, that is; the details don't matter.'

'The essential truth is that you love him and would never leave him.'

'Is that a question? But yes, the answer is yes.'

'I shall ask no more questions today.'

'It will all unfold in its own time.'

'That is the one predictable thing about the future.'

Later, that night, Luke lay in bed and played back in his head the tape of everything they had done and said. He heard her voice, he heard the rustle of the bedclothes, he heard the quiet murmur of the tree outside the window, the lovely robinia, its bare branches stirring in the breeze. He remembered the wild joy, the ecstatic moments, the sheer fun of her company and of how she was in bed. Perhaps a love affair had started; he could not be sure. And then the telephone had brought their encounter to a close. The dressing and gathering of themselves together before their parting had a business-like air about it. Perhaps the two-week rule would be a good fallback, but as yet he could not properly assemble his thoughts. The main memory was the uncontrollable urge that had stormed his senses when their hands touched outside the bedroom door: an urge subdued only by the act of love itself. But was it that? Was it love, or just another case of intemperate desire? He had been aware of an accelerating build-up of interest in this unexpected woman, and had wondered where it might lead. She was, after all, married.

Adultery is best avoided; he had been caught unawares outside that door.

He thought of Wendy, and wondered how much longer that would still hurt. He had been unable to bring up the subject when Penny began her innocent probing the week before. Yes, Wendy Chang was lodged in his memory. Their affair had gone far beyond time. Her beauty had enthralled him, and her sophistication had overwhelmed his normal scepticism of that suspect quality. He was falling ever deeper when it had been forced to an abrupt end. A director of his firm had called him into the office one Monday morning to tell him he had been seen in amorous contact with Wendy Chang the day before, walking on the Peak. The director had been instructed to tell him – without disclosing the source of the instruction – that Ms Chang was the mistress of a highly placed official, a dangerous man with political ambitions and resentment of expatriates. Ms Chang, in short, and not to put too fine a point on it, was a commercial spy, thought to have been employed by that official on several previous occasions. Her job was to extract sensitive financial and personal information from people like himself. Luke was asked if he had been aware of any such attempts on him. He denied it at the time, though later found himself wondering whether he should re-interpret some of their post-coital chatter. It was anyway of no consequence. He had not seen her again. His firm found a good reason to explain the sudden need of his presence, permanently, at their London office. He was offered compensation, if he preferred. That was when Luke quit. He had been bound to secrecy on every aspect of the affair, but was anyway disinclined to talk about an incident that had so hurt his *amour propre*, and left him nursing a sense of betrayal.

He still could not bring himself to accept that Wendy had been so much less than he had imagined her, that she could so easily have deceived him, that she had another, controlling lover, and had behaved so cynically. He went over again and again the way their conversations had developed. Time and again he recalled the hours he had spent in her splendid apartment. It was true, that apartment must have cost more than would be affordable on a reporter's salary. There were other things, signs, hints of another life, of other interests and obligations that he found it difficult to interpret. It had seemed part of her inscrutable charm, a mystery he would have to accept, admire and enjoy. He had admired and enjoyed it all too much.

Penny was a different sort of woman, not just for being English, but for appealing to a different part of him. The gamine in her made him feel younger; her radical bent amused him. But, being serious with himself, he could not see a future for them, and thought she would in time feel the same.

On her way to the village shop, Penny bumped into Harold.
'I have a guest who says he knows you.'
'Oh?'
'A Mr Banfield. Eric, I think he said.'
'It rings a bell. A faint one.'
'Said he saw you in the village yesterday evening. Thought he recognised you. Came in and asked me if there was a Harold Ingram here. I said "Yes". Was I right?'
'Your asking suggests that it might not be. Is there something about him?'
'He doesn't look quite the sort of person who would be a close friend. But perhaps I shouldn't say that.'

'I would trust your judgement, Penny. What does he look like?'

'Shortish, verging on the stout, and nearly bald. His most distinctive feature is a narrow moustache. It looks stuck on.'

'I know him,' Harold said without enthusiasm. 'He was a junior in the High Commission where I'd been posted. West Africa, many years ago. So he still sprouts that ghastly moustache! What is he doing here?'

'He's just retired. No wife. Thinks he'll look around for a house. Perhaps settle here.'

Penny waited for Harold to say something. 'Should I tell him where you live, if he asks?'

'Of course, if he asks. In fact it might be interesting to catch up on things. Send him along, by all means.'

They parted, with Penny wondering about life in the Diplomatic Service.

'Nice place you've got here, Harold, very nice.'

Harold looked at him, and could not remember whether Banfield had previously addressed him by his first name.

'I'm sorry my wife is not here to greet you. She has business in the village. Well then, sit down and tell me what's been happening to you in all these years.'

Eric Banfield spoke at some length of his various postings. Harold had a professional interest in some of the things his visitor told him, but the man's account of his life seemed to concentrate on the personal and the trivial; he had little to say of the diplomatic and political. He talked about the drinking holes he had patronised, and the local women he had consorted with. He gossiped about the local staff in the missions where he had served; what little he said about his British colleagues was mostly scurrilous. There was an ingratiating tone in the way he spoke, especially when talking of the seamier side of his adventures. His moustache bobbed about as though stuck on, as Penny had said. Harold, remembering that he had never much taken to the man, found himself now becoming uncomfortable in his presence.

'Well, Harold, to come back to Africa, you certainly left something behind to remember.' His laugh, as he said this, sounded to Harold like a snigger.

'What on earth do you mean?'

'Well, these things are all fair and square between men, aren't they? I mean, well, it's Esther I'm talking about. I do remember the name. I remember her quite well. Very nice too. I saw a bit of her after you left. Until she had the child. She told me herself it was yours.'

Harold looked stunned. Banfield went on, 'You knew, Harold? You must have known. Surely?' The last word came out in a wheedling tone. Harold looked aghast at the man now writhing in his chair.

'What are you saying, man? Do you sit there telling me after all these years that I fathered a child there? Do you realise what you're saying? Do you have a shred of evidence for any of this? You sit there and snigger over this monstrous allegation as though I were one of your ghastly mates.'

Harold spat out the last two words and stood up. He glowered down at Banfield, who could see that the visit was over. Without a further word, Harold walked through the lobby to the front door, opened it, and waited for his visitor to pass. The man, a mixture of anger and wretchedness, hesitated on the doorstep. As he left he delivered his parting shot.

'All I know is what your Esther told me. That she was having your baby. So don't be your high and mighty self with me, Harold Ingram!' And then he was gone, with a loud bang of the door behind him.

Harold staggered rather than walked back across the room. He put his hands on the mantelpiece over the fireplace, and bowed his head.

'I heard that.'

He spun round. Thelma was in the kitchen doorway. She was as white-faced as he. They stood quite still for a long moment, staring at each other. 'I think you had better do some talking,' she finally said, and they went wretchedly to their armchairs.

'I didn't hear you come back,' he said.

'I got through quicker than expected. I came quietly into the kitchen, wondering when to come in and interrupt. Then I heard him say all that. Is it true, Harold?'

He groaned. 'I don't know. To be honest, as I must be, it could be true. It sounds true. I just don't know.' He spoke slowly and quietly. 'It was the time you came back to England to see Luke into his new school. I was out there for two months on my own; it was before I got the posting to Japan. Esther was available – to put it bluntly. But I should say more than that about her. She was a nice woman, a good woman. Not a tramp. I am thinking of excuses, but what's the point? We met quite often. There could have been a baby, but it never occurred to me there would be. There should not have been. We took the obvious precautions. We parted on good terms; she had always understood I was about to leave, and that would be the end of it. Oh, Thelma! After all these years, for you to be confronted with this! If it's any use, I can give you all the apologies you want. I never loved her, really loved her. I admired her and I liked her. But I have always loved you. That was just an affair. Just a brief, inconsequential affair, something that happens. It happened. It's had no effect on my life – till now. It has had no effect on our marriage. If that awful man had never come, neither of us would ever have known about it.'

'You sit there talking as though you can just talk your way out of it, and then I suppose you'll think we can go on as though nothing had happened. Well it *has* happened. The skeleton has come crashing out of your cupboard, and we've got to think of what to do about it. I've got to think what I must do about it.'

They sat in silence for a time, till Thelma said, 'I don't want to see you until tomorrow morning. I want to think. I want to be on my own. I shall go for a walk. When I get back please be out of my sight. You can sleep in the bedroom. I shall use the spare room. If you want to eat you can find something. We will talk in the morning. On no account must anyone else know about this, Harold. Not Luke, not anyone. Unless that dreadful man talks. We will consider all this tomorrow.'

Harold kept a tactical silence, while his wife of forty-five years crossed the room, put on a coat in the lobby, and closed the front door quietly behind her.

They lay, that night, aware of their separate ceilings.

Harold, in the long reaches before sleep, thought of many things. Two big things stood out for him. Somewhere in the world, perhaps in that hot corner of Africa where he had been all those years ago, there was a child of his, now an adult, a man or a woman, who would know no more of him than the mother had wanted to tell. The other thought was how devastated Thelma had been at the news. He desperately hoped she would soon recover from this exposure of an ancient infidelity. It was bad, of course, it was very bad, but they must put it in perspective. He hoped they could come to focus on their common problem: how to come to terms with the existence of that other person.

The incident, the affair, his fall from grace if that is what it was, all that was thirty-one years ago. It might now seem really so little, so ancient. His thoughts kept returning to that long-past period, half a lifetime ago. So much had changed since then. He had changed; he and Thelma had grown older and wiser, growing and changing together, achieving mutual tolerance and unquestioning attachment, maintaining all that while the world changed. And yet in looking back he saw himself as the same person. Even as a child, looking at the world with the eyes and mind of a child, making the simple judgements of a child, it was always he, Harold Ingram, who had done the seeing, the thinking and the judging. And in all the years since, it had always been he, the same he, who had done and thought all the various things that constituted his life. A person was like a river, never composed of quite the same particles from one moment to the next, yet keeping its singular nature. The body renewed its many cells every seven years, he had heard. At seventy-six he must have replaced himself almost eleven times. A river was no more than an indentation on the surface of the earth, a conduit for the flow of water performing its perennial cycle from sea to sky to hills and back to sea. A river is a process, not a substance. Is that the way to see one's life? Is our ever-changing body no more than a conduit for the events that pass through it? The pursuit of a career, falling in love and making a marriage, having and rearing a son, scholarship, prowess, all the achievements and all the failures of common ambition, what is the thread that holds all these together so that one can look back and call it one's life?

Harold, lying on his back, wrestled with his thoughts and did not try to sleep. He came back to the same thought, the common thread to it all. Quite simply: consciousness. His and his alone. However much, however frequently he may have changed, there was a single thread of consciousness that could take him back to every part of his life, and return him to where he was, and it was always him, uniquely and only him, doing the looking and the thinking. The essential him: a solitary moral agent in and of his life. That moral agent had started as a seed, it had grown and matured with experience, it had acted and been acted upon. Perhaps this was what Christians call the soul, except the soul was supposed to come from somewhere else, and then pass on to eternity. But never mind the soul. Consciousness has a moral dimension. Man is responsible for his actions. I am responsible for that child. I must accept that responsibility. Oh, God, let me just think about it, let me have time to think what I have to do. I will decide. I just need time.

So, in looking back at this past affair, he knew it was no excuse to say he had been a different person then. The person who decided and acted as he had done then was the person lying in bed now looking at the ceiling, which was reflecting a pale moonlight coming through the windows that he had left uncurtained.

Thoughts, memories came thrusting in. Trapped in a fusillade, targeted from all directions, he searched for a sense of Thelma, lying in the other room. What was she thinking?

He told himself the story. Port Stephen had at first been a good posting. The town was bright and bursting with the euphoria that followed Independence. The people were bright, and the streets had a bustling gaiety. There was plenty to keep him busy in his job, setting up contacts for business and advising on the new development programmes from the government back home. But towards the end of his three-year stint, the practical difficulties of doing business of any sort were becoming more evident. And the climate, in a part of the world once called the white man's grave, was affecting even his strong constitution. He was glad when the next posting, to Japan, came in sight. He would have a short spell back home, with a briefing in London and then a spot of leave. But a few weeks before all that came up, Luke got chicken pox at his prep school in England. It was the end of his last term before going on to public school, and Thelma had gone home early for his convalescence. Harold had been left on his own to finish his job and see to the packing up.

He remembered well the sense of exhaustion and of endless humid heat. He remembered the sense of disruption that came from his sudden solitary state. Friends and colleagues had rallied round, and the diplomatic circuit offered its usual social diversions. It was at one of these that he had got to know Esther. They had already met, in the office of the Scandinavian aid agency where she worked. He had had to send back a report on what the agency was doing. Esther had helped him. Now the Scandinavians were throwing a party, to which Mr and Mrs Ingram were invited. Harold went alone.

Esther came up to him at the party, and soon they were sitting down together with a drink, and learning more about each other. She was the daughter of a Lebanese father and a Persian mother. The father had been a successful trader, like many others along that stretch of African coast. He had died, leaving her mother with sufficient money to live comfortably and to continue the education of their daughter. She had graduated from the American University of Beirut, and had no difficulty in finding a position of responsibility back in Port Stephen. Her mother was the daughter of parents who had left Persia before it became Iran, and would continue to see themselves as Persian. Esther too had been brought up to see herself in that light, being named after the ancient queen of that great country. For Harold the old name conjured up images of beauty and splendour, as it must have done for this young woman's expatriate parents. But it struck him quite forcibly that Esther needed no enhancements of glamorous heritage to add lustre to her own remarkable beauty. The blend of parentage had resulted in something exquisite, quite unlike anything he had seen in other women.

When he got to know her better, he probed to see why she had not married. She was in her early thirties, ten or so years younger than him. Surely she had had proposals, opportunities? There was the local community of her parents, of which he knew little except that it held itself aloof from the African people; and there was the diplomatic community, with plenty of well-paid and eligible young men having promising careers in front of them. Someone must have caught her eye?

She was not the sort of woman to give a direct answer to questions of that nature. She spoke on the subject of men generally. She gave him the impression of strong independence, and a general disdain for most of the men she had met. Harold could not help feeling flattered to be so well regarded by this superior creature.

It had seemed to start innocently enough; but the mixture of heat, solitude, and the drinking that went with it, was potent. Esther was a source of ease for him. They walked in quiet places and were comfortable with each other; mostly she talked to him, and he liked listening to her soft Persian voice. Soon they were making love. He had made it clear on that first occasion that there could be no future for them. He would leave quite soon and never see her again. Nor would he write. She said she understood. She would be sad when he went, but glad that they had known each other. She knew how to settle for what came her way, and to make her own future. She had said something like that, and he tried hard now, in his present bedroom, to remember more clearly what exactly she had said.

He sat up with a jolt when a thought occurred to him. Had she wanted his child? Had she just wanted a child and used him for that purpose? He knew it sometimes happened like that, and he saw her as capable of wanting it and doing it. Had she deceived him about their contraception? She was not careless and certainly not stupid. She had always struck him as a woman totally in control of herself. He lay down and looked at the possibility. His thoughts ranged forward. He looked at the course of his subsequent life and tried to imagine the course of an unknown parallel life in that tiny West African state. Another thought sprung at him. Luke, all these years, had had a half-brother or half-sister. Quite possibly he is now an uncle. Should he tell Luke? It would seem right to do so. He must first discuss that with Thelma. His thoughts ranged again, up and down the river of his life. It was becoming an obsessive metaphor. He looked thirty-one years upstream and saw a new rocky outcrop; the waters split and rushed round it; the disturbance came all the way downstream; the waters rushed around his feet and he could hear the roar of them as he fell asleep.

After he left Harold that afternoon, Eric Banfield walked quickly back to *Coralita*. His anger and humiliation made him determined to pack up and return to London by the next train: to hell with house hunting in this wretched place. He must find Mrs Hall and announce his early departure. She was not to be seen. He packed in readiness and feeling in need of cigarettes went to the village shop. Coming out he bumped into a woman going in. She was a tall, commanding woman in her early to mid-fifties. Her hair was flecked with grey; her clothes were those of a sensible countrywoman. Hermione Bodleigh, spinster of this Parish and clerk to its Council, gave him an appraising eye. She observed his good shoes and gold watch.

After apologising, Banfield asked her, 'Is there a bus to St Giles, do you know? Or if not, where can I get a taxi?'

'There is no bus today, but you'll find the number of the local taxi service in the shop window here. Where is it you want to go?'

'I must get the next train to London. First I have to see Mrs Hall at *Coralita* to settle my account. I can't find her.'

Miss Bodleigh made a clucking sound, suggestive of disapproval. She saw that he was agitated. She made a decision.

'The next train is at five forty-seven. I am going into St Giles, I have something to collect. I can drop you at the station. There is plenty of time, and if Mrs Hall is not there, you can leave a note for her. Will that be all right for you?'

'More than all right. It's very kind of you.'

'Then I will pick you up at Mrs Hall's in ten minutes.'

Hermione walked round the corner to the terraced cottage house she shared with another single woman. 'Ethel, something has come up. I have to go into town. I shall be back by six-thirty.'

Hermione was back at six-twenty, having hurried straight home after dropping her charge at the station.

'Ethel!' she exclaimed, 'Would you believe it!'

At six o'clock the next morning Harold took a tray of tea into the room where Thelma had spent the night.

'Whatever we have to say to each other, we should start the day with a cup of tea. We are English and we are married.'

'Yes, Harold. We have been married forty-five years. I have spent the night thinking of it.'

Harold dispensed the tea, and sat in the chair by the window. He waited.

'I have been thinking of it through the night,' Thelma went on, 'a night I hope never to repeat. This thing of yours happened many years ago. That does not lessen the shock of it. It throws the whole of our married life into a new perspective. Tom was right, about skeletons in cupboards. A lot of mutual history must now be re-written. Everything that has happened since that moment of betrayal carries the stain of it; it can never be washed away. I know these things happen. I just never thought they would happen to me, to us. If it ever crossed my mind to think of your fidelity, I just took it for granted. Other women's husbands might do that sort of thing, but not mine. And now I have to confront my stupid innocence.'

Harold remained quiet, waiting.

'Of course, I wonder about the woman. You say it was a casual affair, but you just can't treat people like that. You don't share my religion, but we surely share a common moral code. You are responsible for your actions. You are responsible to that poor woman. And you are, above all, responsible for any child you have fathered, in or out of marriage.'

Harold now spoke. 'I too spent the night thinking. You must not suppose I am unaware of the moral issue, but solutions to problems of this sort do not spring ready-made out of one night's thinking. I have turned over and over every side of the question; I remain shocked and indecisive; I am unable to compose myself. I see my younger self in a more tolerant light than you do. That perhaps is a man's point of view. But I recognise that yours is different, and I have to respect it. It is not for me, now, to look back at that time and say "No, I should not have done it." That is not a solution. I did it. My main problem now, is how to help you regain your trust in me. We have had all these years of marriage. They cannot be sacrificed because of one misdeed so long ago. It has been a good marriage. I have seen few better. We must find a way to deal with this setback. Let us continue as best we can and wait for calm to return. It has taken us too much by surprise. We must be quiet. Too much talking is worse than too little. Let us think. I am thinking of that child, if indeed there was one. The child would now be thirty or so years of age, and has probably had children that are now my grandchildren. What am I to do about it?'

'I too have been wondering. I believe you have to find out, one way or the other. Was there a child, and if so what happened to it? If necessary you must go back and ask.'

'I expect you are right.'

'Harold, I have been shocked and hurt. Deeply hurt. Are we talking of an isolated incident? Was that the only one, the only time you've been unfaithful? I must know. You must tell me the truth.'

'Thelma, my darling wife. There has been no other time. No

other woman. I never wanted to be unfaithful, even that once, I did not consciously choose infidelity. But it happened. I did not stop it from happening. I saw it then as a temporary comfort at a taxing time. I saw it as something that I could put behind me when it was over. Which I did, and I have never repeated it.'

Thelma's reply was very soft; Harold had to lean forward to hear her. 'If that is true, Harold, you may come into my bed and comfort me. I am the one who needs it.'

As he took his wife into his arms, he felt the dampness on her cheeks, and saw it in her eyes. It prompted a response in his own.

Later, at breakfast, Harold said to his wife, 'I must tell Luke. He ought to know. Somewhere in the world he may have a brother or sister'.

'I will leave you to tell him. But you are right. He should know. Tell him I want him to know.'

Harold phoned his son after breakfast, and was invited for coffee. Father and son now sat by the window, the coffee tray between them.

'Luke, my boy, I am in the doghouse.'

'It is man's common habitation.'

'I do not mean to joke. I will come straight to the point. You remember as a boy when you had chicken pox and your mother came back to look after you? I was on my own for a while, in Port Stephen. It was before my move to Japan. Well, in those last few weeks I had an affair. I won't make excuses for it, though God knows one can be driven to these things. We had an understanding, she and I, that it would be no more than a temporary liaison. All very civilised, you know. If I have thought of her since, it is as a one-time friend, in the way one sometimes makes friends overseas, then leaves the friendship behind. There was never any question of your mother being replaced in my affections. Your mother is the only woman I have ever loved.'

Harold had been speaking slowly and deliberately. Luke, initially inquisitive, was now concerned at the signs of his father's distress.

'The past has caught up with me. It has caught me unawares. A junior colleague of mine, from the High Commission out there, has turned up in the village, staying at Penny's; he saw me in the street and finished up on my doorstep. This was yesterday. He was never a friend of mine, but I had no reason not to be sociable. I asked him in, and he threw this bombshell at me. He told me I had fathered a child out there.'

Harold paused. Luke filled in the silence, 'After all these years! Was Ma there to hear the man?'

'Not in the room. But she had come into the kitchen the back way, and just happened to hear that crucial bit at the end, before I got rid of him. I won't tell you everything that was said between us, after that. She was devastated, as you may imagine. But we are coming round. We shall come round. I am convinced. We have been together so many years. This thing was a long, long time ago. But it will haunt, you know, it will haunt. What I have to say to you, Luke, my son, my boy, is that I must acknowledge the possible existence of another child, a brother or sister to you. I cannot tell you yet what I think I ought to do about it, or what I am likely to do about it. But it is something you ought to know, and your mother said I was to tell you she wanted you to know.'

Luke wondered what to say first.

'I can see it cost you something to tell me, but I'm glad you have.

Let me assure you, Pa, I do not judge you for what happened. You have lived longer than I have, but I think I have seen more of the modern world than you, since you retired. I see these things from a less rigid perspective, which is perhaps why you judge yourself in a way that I would not.' Harold snorted, but Luke continued, 'We will not talk about right and wrong. There is a practical question. You should not think it upsets me to hear that I may have a brother or sister. It's a slightly disturbing thought, but also an intriguing one. The practical question is of course what to do about it. If I may ask: why is it, do you suppose, that the lady in question has concealed it from you all these years? What could have been her reason?'

'I have been asking myself that very question. The only thing I can think is that she wanted a child all along. Let me tell you, Luke, you were right to call her a lady. She was a fine woman, interesting, cultured, intelligent.'

Luke avoided raising his eyebrows at the accolade, though he recognised its value for self-respect.

'It is early days, of course, but have you thought of trying to make contact with her again? And how should we refer to her?'

'Her name was Esther. I will tell you more in due course. But yes, to answer your question, I have been wondering about that. It will not be easy for me at my age, but I think I must do something to find out more.'

'Let us all do some thinking. We must include mother in that, mustn't we?'

'Yes, we must.'

Harold got up to go. 'Thank you, Luke. I feel better for our talk. Now I must get back.'

A few days later, Dorothy was sitting in Jean's kitchen, for the second 'troika' meeting. They had to put the finishing touches to their proposals for the summer solstice party. Thelma had rung them that morning to say that Harold was unwell and needed her attention. She had asked Hermione Bodleigh to take her place.

'Hermione should be used to taking minutes. She is Parish clerk, after all,' said Dorothy.

'Exactly!' said Jean, 'you can give her those notes you took last time, and she can write everything up after our session this morning.'

Hermione joined them a moment later. Jean brought coffee and a homemade cake to the table. 'Pleasure before work!' she said.

'It was short notice for you this morning,' Dorothy said to the newcomer.

'Yes, but I was free. I hope Harold has nothing serious. He has had his worries lately.'

'Worries?' asked Dorothy.

'Well, I don't think I'm speaking out of turn, but it seems a past affair has come to light. There was a child he knew nothing about. Abroad, it was. Fancy finding that out, at his age. I wonder what his wife thinks of it.'

'Are you sure of this, Hermione? How did it come to light?'

'Quite by chance. I gave a lift into St Giles to a man who had known Harold in Africa, at the time of the incident. He'd just seen Harold again, in the village. He told me all about it. He was quite sure. Of course, we shouldn't talk about this to all and sundry.'

The other two considered this injunction.

Dorothy said, 'I shall have to tell Tom. The Ingrams are such close friends. Tom ought to know, in case he can help.'

Jean said, 'These things have a way of getting out. But I will tell Michael not to breathe a word. Who else have you told, Hermione?'

Hermione shifted on her seat. 'I told Ethel, naturally. But she is the soul of discretion. Now, shouldn't we be getting down to business?'

They went through the six proposals drafted at the first meeting. Dorothy found it difficult to concentrate, thinking all the time of Thelma and wondering how she would cope. Jean did most of the talking, having been primed with ideas by Michael. Hermione was efficient at putting the ideas into clear proposals for submission to Michael's sub-committee.

'That's all done, then,' said Jean at the end.

Dorothy reminded them, 'We have one more session, just before the party. When we know who's bought tickets, we have to do a seating plan. I expect Thelma will want to be in on that, Hermione.'

'Of course. So long as Ethel and I can sit together,' she replied.

The Reverend Tom Foster, fifty-four years of age, came of a generation that would have assumed he was christened correctly as Thomas. So far as the villagers knew, he had always been Tom and liked to be addressed as such. He and his wife Dorothy, four years younger, were known for their generosity, both in pastoral work and in domestic entertaining. The latter was of a quality suggesting financial resources beyond a normal stipend. Tom was aware that some of his younger colleagues, especially those in urban parishes, referred to him as a 'gentleman rector'. He disregarded what he may have felt to be the unchristian attitude behind these remarks. His parishioners, high and low, knew him as a man of no side. Physically, he was short and round, seeming to approximate as close as a person can to a spherical form. He would say that this was how he came to be lacking in side. He knew that his old-fashioned approach to his work, as a 'gentleman rector', would keep him in his present incumbency. This did not distress him. He was on good terms with his bishop, but knew he would not be preferred. Nothing could dent his good nature, which shone as a beacon on believer and unbeliever alike. He talked a lot, which pleased Dorothy; she was a good woman, who did good works quietly.

It had become a custom with them to entertain friends to dinner on an evening shortly after Easter. This year their guests were the three Ingrams and the two Halls. It was mid-April and Dorothy had filled vases with tulips from the garden. The mahogany table they sat round was circular, making the seven of them feel in equal contact with each other. The table was adorned with Tom's family silver, Wedgwood china and old wine glasses. There had been a good white Loire with the first course, and now they were enjoying claret with the lamb.

Luke, aware of his parents' sombre mood, had been making an effort at lightness.

'I saw an extraordinary sight in the village this morning,' he said, 'two people came pedalling past, lying down on strange contraptions, and looking like decayed royalty. There were flagpoles attached, with something indecipherable waving limply from the top.'

'That was Michael and Jean you saw', Dorothy told him, 'and those contraptions are bicycles called "recumbents". They are said to be very good for you. Michael and Jean swear by them. He will talk about it non-stop if you let him. And the flagpoles carry emblems of their various green causes. It is a way to advertise them. Greenery is their religion, replacing the true one, I'm afraid.'

'Too much enthusiasm is bad for the soul,' said Tom, holding up and gazing with pleasure into his wine, 'except of course for the things that really matter. I have been re-reading Strachey's *Victorians*,' he continued, after taking a sip. 'His piece on Manning starts with a sketch of the life that a man of the Church led, in those days before doctrine and dissent disturbed the peace. Portly parsons rode to hounds in the morning, and consumed their two bottles of an evening. Ah, well, I suppose we should not regret that those days have passed. Not many of us would have the liver for those two bottles a night. Of course, Strachey had rather more to say about his subject than that. You're the historian, Harold, what's your view of him?'

'Who, Strachey? My tutor at Oxford told me to read him. Not because the history was right – historians tend not to say that of other historians, which Strachey wasn't anyway – but because the book itself had become history. The assault on eminence by irony – or you might prefer to call it sarcasm – was one of the ways history came to be written by non-historians. Great fun, of course. And I was taught that literary style was of major importance in the writing of history. That too became history, though I must admit there are now signs of its resurrection. But Strachey certainly had style in spades. My tutor was right.'

'I had an enlightened English tutor at Keele who told me to read Strachey for the same reason,' said Penny. 'And I think, now, *Eminent Victorians* would be a suitable work for Media Studies'. Harold snorted. 'Well', Penny continued, 'it's the literary precursor of what so many television programmes do, when a non-professional puts a "human" journalistic slant on a subject, often to rubbish a person's reputation.'

'Iconoclasm for its own sake,' said Rupert. 'Well, we don't have eminences anymore, to be pulled off their pedestals. More's the pity. Only celebrities, with their very transient glory. True eminence is out of fashion, apart from the grey sort, lurking in Whitehall. But, Tom, to revert to Manning and that lot. They went Catholic, didn't they? Now, I have been taking instruction from a Jesuit friend in London. I have been a Protestant atheist all my sensible life, as you know. But I have to tell you, I am considering going over. I find Catholic atheism so much more respectable, intellectually. Catholics take their doctrine seriously.'

'My dear Rupert,' Tom replied, 'we shall of course be sorry to lose you, but I must warn you of error. Catholics take their doctrine too seriously. Your Jesuit friend may provide you with entertaining intellectual games, but you should never lose sight of the greater importance of simple faith, the sort of faith that is there for all, whatever their mental capacity. Think hard, I say, before relinquishing the well-tried, Anglican atheism. And one day you may find the true faith.'

'Well said, Tom,' Thelma intervened. 'I have been wanting comfort from the old virtues.' She spoke quietly, in a tone of voice that made the others stop to look at her.

'Thelma is alluding to my recent problem,' Harold said. 'There is no need to be secret about it. The whole village knows. A man from my past came to this village for two nights, and might as well have pinned the story on the village notice board. I am almost a celebrity, though it is not the sort of celebrity I cherish. Men come up to me in the street and, without saying anything too obvious, make it clear they think me quite a character, an old dog, one of them, conforming to a model of what a man ought to be. It is a strange way for a man to win respect. The women are different. I get quite an old-fashioned look from many of them. Well, as of course you know, it seems I must have fathered a child in Africa thirty-one years ago. This was complete news to me. I have to believe it, until I'm able to confirm it one way or the other. That I must do. You have been good in not pressing me on the subject, but the subject presses on me; and on Thelma, my dear wife of all these years.'

Tom replied to this. 'Harold, it's true about the rumour-mongering, and I have tried to discourage it. But you can't stop it. It is simple human nature, and in itself means no ill. But I'm glad you have spoken. I am here for you to talk to, as you know, if ever you want to – but for now I think we should continue with an easier subject over dinner. Dorothy has been slaving in the kitchen all afternoon, and dessert is still to come. Luke, I'm told you have been seen with a tennis racquet?'

'That sounds like a question. Perhaps you think it out of character. Penny clearly thinks so.' They exchanged glances, observed by Rupert. 'But I like to think that I only look like a weedy layabout. Occasionally I take a little exercise; and the club's standard is not too strenuous.'

Dorothy asked him, 'Can we come to see you playing?'

'You would be very welcome to see me playing, Dorothy, but you might be disappointed to see my playing.'

'Oh, I do like to hear a good gerund,' said Harold, 'If I have done nothing else, I have instilled a sense of grammar in my son.'

'Like father like son,' said Dorothy, displaying a fondness for each.

'The neglect of the gerund marks the decline of Western civilisation,' Harold proclaimed, sounding as though he meant it.

'Yes, and how splendid of you to remind us, Harold,' said Rupert. 'Let no one decry pedantry: it is the great solace of the solitary man.' He was looking across the table, in the space between Luke and Penny, as he continued, 'And we must hope that Luke does not remain solitary for long. I am inclined to ask you all to stand for a toast: "Long live the gerund!" But let us take it as drunk. It is at moments like this that one appreciates the importance of the trivial. Do you know, there is a bare half-dozen mentions of that word in the *Oxford Dictionary of Quotations*? I looked it up the other day. It is strange that so few great minds should have found anything memorable to say on such an important topic. Strange, when one thinks of all the trivial things that consume so much of our attention. They are the things that provide the essential backdrop to thought, like the all-important wall or curtain behind a painted portrait. Trivia, you could say, are the essential ingredient in most people's conversation. And if you recognise, as I'm sure you do, my use of the Latin plural, I shall thank you for your trivium. One of the trivial things I sometimes remember is something a boy at school had written on a desk. It was: "and he differentiated". He would have been fifteen or sixteen, and just starting the differential calculus. Imagine! He was so enthralled at the heroic efforts of someone – himself, presumably – grappling with this mathematical mystery, that he felt impelled to immortalise the action with this message on the desk. It conjures up a picture, an aquatint, as I see it, in an oval, mahogany frame; the edges of the print are obscure but the light reveals a boy in the centre, sitting with his elbow on a desk, one hand on his head, the other holding a pen. Numbers and symbols cover the paper in front of him. And then comes the climactic moment! He differentiates!'

'Thank you, Rupert,' Dorothy said, 'you deserve a place of your own in the Oxford Quotations. We shall never again regard the trivial as merely that. And you have so eloquently filled the gap between dessert and coffee.'

When they had all moved back to the sitting-room, and comfortably spread themselves in their chairs, Dorothy spoke. 'Times have changed all right!' she said, perhaps following an unexpressed line of thought. 'I often wonder what my father would have made of the modern age. Harold, I suppose your father would have been the oldest of our respective forebears, the eldest among our elders. What do you think he would have made of it?'

'God knows! Not much, I think.' Harold settled himself again, as though preparing for a lengthy recollection of his deceased parent.

'My father was an Edwardian. He came to manhood in the first decade of the new century, after the great queen had died and a lighter touch was felt in national life. He was there, to enjoy it. But he had been brought up in a Victorian household, and certain values and standards never left him. His father before him came of yeoman stock; he had married well, and done well in business. With moderate wealth, and my grandmother's help, he became a gentleman. My father went one better, being the first in the family to go to university, and then enter the ranks of the professional classes. He achieved some eminence as a doctor, with rooms close to Harley Street. You might say he was a second generation English gentleman, imbued from birth with that ethos, and accepting as a matter of course all the privileges and responsibilities that came with the status. It was a status marked by dress, manners and deportment. One's position in the world was demonstrated by speech and by modes of address, being scrupulous in marking the distinction between superiors and inferiors. And my father's generation, you must understand, his colleagues and his social circle, saw themselves as liberal and enlightened. Compared with their forebears, they were. Both as individuals and as citizens, they accepted some responsibility for the poor. But above all, I think what marked the English gentleman of the period was his attitude to his womenfolk. When my father married, his bride came with a virginity guaranteed by her class and upbringing. Needless to say, the man's was not. Of course, none of this was mentioned. It didn't have to be. But a maiden's virginity, in the purely anatomical aspect, was part of a more general inexperience, an unsullied innocence, seen by father and husband as something precious to be preserved. Men were the protectors of their women, shielding them from the wicked world beyond the garden gate. The depravities that are now splashed across every daily newspaper were then hidden. This really was a second age of chivalry. And my parents were a truly devoted couple, right to the end. Perhaps it helped that they did not see too much of each other. He spent most of the week in London, leaving my mother to look after us children in our Hertfordshire suburb – with the help of servants, I might add. And his life was almost exclusively masculine, in a way we have forgotten. From his school, through university and into professional life, he lived and worked with men. At his London club he talked only to men. For the gentlemen of that era, the opposite sex entered their lives in one of two mutually exclusive ways: they met ladies on social occasions, as wives, daughters or mothers; and for what they saw as entertainment they met women who might not be ladies, elsewhere, with families absent. I don't know what my father got up to, I can only guess. But I know he regarded his home as a shrine, for his devotion to my mother. And there were many things that could not be spoken of there, things that for a doctor and a man of the world, as he was, would be a part of his daily experience and masculine conversation. But her purity of mind was to be preserved from all that, by a wall of ignorance. Of course she must have heard of things, events, lawsuits and so on. She could not have been as ignorant as he wanted to imagine. But if she asked him an awkward question, he deflected it. When he heard my brother and me discussing the Oscar Wilde trial, he told us not to talk of such things in our mother's house. But when he and I talked of it later, elsewhere, he expressed sympathy with Wilde's predicament. For him, there was a language of the world, and a language of chivalry, for the home, each with its distinct vocabulary. No one else would know or could imagine what they might say to each other, in their most intimate moments, but those bedroom words would not be uttered in the other rooms of the house.

'I don't know how much of all that has come down to me. I don't even see myself as a gentleman, in the way my father would have wanted. I expect he would be disappointed in me. I accept, indeed I welcome, the role of women in modern life. And if they don't miss the pedestal, we should not force them onto one. But I think we all gain, as husbands and wives, by giving protection to our life-partners. The principle of mutual protection is the right one for any age.'

There was desultory conversation after that, of late departed parents, and of days gone by. But by this stage hosts and guests were ready for their beds.

Thelma and Harold walked home in slightly less sober mood than when they had set out earlier. But for Thelma the evening had not quite finished.

'When you were talking about your father,' she said, 'I couldn't help wondering what he would have made of your present predicament. You have not been successful in protecting your wife from knowledge of your illegitimate child.'

'Yes, I wonder what he would have done. Perhaps if I had followed his lead, I would never have opened my door to the likes of Mr Banfield. Then neither of us would have known. But that is the difference. I am more of a democrat than my father.'

'You are not talking like one.'

Harold decided to leave it at that.

The next morning, Luke went to see his parents.

'Ma, Pa, I have been thinking. Somewhere in the world – and where, we don't know – I have a half-brother or -sister. I should like to know which. Should I think of a "him" or a "her"? You must feel the same. We really have to find out. I must confess, I am intrigued by the whole possibility. You mustn't mind my putting it so personally, but I would really like to meet my sibling. I won't say whether I'd prefer a him or a her,' – and he thought of his recently acquired mock-sister, Penny – 'because I shall not know until I have seen who it is. Then I shall know.' He was looking alternately at his mother and father as he spoke. They remained silent but restive, as if gathering their respective thoughts. 'You too have said you have to find out. I've been wondering, from what you have said, whether you would want to make that journey yourself, Pa. I don't think you should. It would be strenuous. It might be distressing. It could well be fruitless. I should go.'

He waited for their reaction.

'My boy, you've spoken with a good feeling. I do want to know, to know it all; as does your mother.' Thelma nodded. 'I have been thinking of the journey. I confess I would not relish the idea, but I have thought it necessary. I think it's for me to go. But I thank you for the offer.'

'Harold, you should reconsider. You are not as fit as you were. Luke is right, it would be physically arduous, and you are too deeply involved to meet that woman again. Luke would have the advantage of being a third party. He would be more objective, appraising the situation.' She turned to her son. 'Have you thought of how you'd set about getting there and finding her?'

'I have time on my hands. I could fly out soon. I would plan to spend up to two weeks there, if necessary, but you would have to give me some leads, Pa. This would be a start. More might be needed.'

'Let me think about it. Your mother and I will talk some more. I see the sense in what you're both saying. Leave it for now. And thank you again.'

At breakfast the following morning, Harold and Thelma agreed they should accept Luke's offer. He would be a good ambassador.

The sprawling capital city of Port Stephen had a large, modern outer perimeter, with faded bungalows, factories and shacks. And there was an old colonial centre, built around the port, where visitors could find the presidential palace, the central bank, most of the ministries and a few shopping streets. Here also was the New Africa Hotel, itself a colonial relic and formerly called the Victoria. It had been well maintained by the local business community, who were its main source of custom. Visitors, mostly business people and officials, were not the sort to seek much else in Port Stephen; no one had yet thought of this country as a tourist destination. It made its way in the world as an *entrepôt* for its less entrepreneurial neighbours. City and country were named after the national hero, Stephen, a slave who had led a revolt at the moment of his embarkation. He had been immortalised since Independence by a statue at the site of his savage slaughter. Luke was looking at it now, from the first-floor bar of the hotel, as he waited for Esther, whom he had finally tracked down under the name of Mrs Abou-Khalid.

He had followed up the several leads that his father had given him. None of the contacts had known Esther, though one or two had known of her. He was given further contacts that might help. Eventually someone had telephoned with a number for the woman who might be the one he wanted. He called the number and found himself speaking to his father's former mistress. It was a difficult moment for both of them; for Esther it must have been an unwelcome surprise. He had been impressed by her poise on the line, and awaited her now with interest and a certain trepidation. He had said only that he had come to Port Stephen with a message from his father Harold Ingram, and he hoped he could pass it to her in person. That was yesterday; he had spent today walking around, reading and fidgeting. She would be at the hotel in ten minutes. He sat waiting in the lounge bar.

It was a quiet place at six in the evening; several small groups had gathered for a drink before dinner, to talk about business or the lesser affairs of state. Its clientele would once have been limited to the white ruling class. There were now people of many nationalities and colours, though mostly African and Asian. Almost all were men. There were many black waiters, some of them of the type of faithful old retainer who might even remember those they had served before

Independence. He saw a Japanese businessman talking earnestly to an African; he heard a German accent at another table; and beyond there was a group of colourfully dressed Africans enjoying each other's company. It was a large room, with comfortable sofas and armchairs well spaced out for privacy. There were large windows giving a view of the port and the open sea beyond. It was a room that would have seen many deals done and fates sealed.

Luke had found a table with two chairs, in a corner where they would be quiet. There was a view of the hotel lobby through the window beside him. As the time came up to six o'clock he watched for her arrival. There was no mistaking her when she walked in from the street. He was on his feet, nodded to his waiter who would keep the table, and was down the stairs in a moment.

They stood a little apart, for a few silent seconds, as she recognised him and took in what she saw. What he saw was a woman whose past beauty had matured into a quiet if slightly dimmed elegance. Her once jet-black hair had grey strands and the sallow complexion of her face had lines. She was dressed well and with little ornamentation, but Luke could see that her clothes were not new. Luke knew her to be in her early sixties, and he admired her upright carriage. He thought his father had shown good taste.

'I would have known you to be Harold's son.'

He felt she meant it as a compliment. 'How would you like me to address you?'

'Please call me Esther. And I can call you Luke.'

He took her upstairs, telling her he remembered the hotel from when his father had brought him here as a boy, visiting from school. They spoke neutrally until their drinks were on the table in front of them, and the waiter had withdrawn.

'I think I should come straight to the point, as to why I'm here. My father had a visit recently from someone he had known in the High Commission when he was working here. He was told something that gave him … a shock'. Luke was looking very closely at Esther as he spoke, to see whether she was anticipating him. 'I wonder whether you know what I'm referring to?'

'You had better say exactly what you mean.'

'He was told that he had fathered a child, and that you were the mother.'

She looked at him for a moment in silence.

'I thought that would be why you came. Who was this visitor your father had?'

'A Mr Banfield. Eric Banfield.'

'Him!' It was said with dislike. 'I remember that man. He pestered me, after your father left. He gave me too much to drink one night, and got me to be more explicit than I should have been, about my relationship with your father. He made me angry and I must have said something that confirmed his supposition. To have surfaced now! After all this time! Poor Harold! And your poor mother! I am truly very sorry. And it was all so unnecessary. I was determined that Harold should never know. But it is true. I had his child.'

There was a further moment of silence, while they looked at their untouched drinks on the table.

'Luke, I think I should tell you about it. Heaven knows you have come far enough for the truth. You shall have the truth. I wanted Harold's child. I won't expect his legitimate son to forgive me for that. No, say nothing yet,' she told him, as he made to reply, 'let me finish. I wanted a child. I did not want to marry. To be frank, I have always preferred the company of women. So I knew I would never have a husband, despite the promptings of my mother. In the society I have lived in, life is difficult for unmarried mothers. They are regarded as outcasts. I could not think of a decent, local man, a man I could respect, among those I knew, to give me a baby without my marrying him. I had met your father; perhaps he has told you how that came about?' Luke nodded. 'I liked him. I admired him. He was the type of man I thought could give me a child to be proud of. I deceived him, I have to admit, by planning it carefully without his knowing. But why should he have had the worry and responsibility for a child that I wanted but he did not? I knew he was due to leave Port Stephen and would probably never return. I took a year off work, and had my baby in Beirut where I had friends. I came back here with a married name and the story that my husband had died. I found a similar job where I had worked before, and various other jobs after that. I have been an honourable widow and supported myself. I had a daughter, a lovely child, and was able to support her too. Now, you may say what you have to say.'

'I have nothing to say at the moment, only questions to ask. Your daughter is my sister.'

'Was your sister, Luke. Oh dear, what a dreadful story I have to tell you. Hannah was just sixteen when she was raped, here in Port Stephen. She died in childbirth.'

'Oh!' was all that came out of Luke's mouth, a soft, low cry, as he thought of the sister he would never know. And finally, 'But there was a child?'

'Yes. A son. He is now fourteen. He goes to school here. It is not as good as I should like, but I had to stop working when I turned sixty, and it is the best I can do for him. He is a clever boy; he will get on well when he is a man. He is lucky in that. God knows who his father was.'

'Esther, your grandson is my father's grandson and my nephew. What is his name?'

'It was for me to name him. I called him John.' She paused, considering, and continued, 'I may as well tell you: I named him after you. I knew from what Harold had told me that he had a son called Luke. John's gospel follows Luke's. I am a Christian, as I hope you are.'

'No, and nor is my father. My mother is the believer. But I am touched by what you've said.'

They continued to talk for some time, adding detail to the story and discussing how Luke would spend the rest of his time in Port Stephen. He was determined to meet John, though Esther was at first reluctant. It was finally agreed that he should come the following evening. They made their arrangements, but Luke could see that Esther had a further question that she was trying to frame. It came out.

'And your mother, Luke. How has she taken all this?'

'She was, as you may imagine, deeply hurt. They have been married forty-five years. They've had a good marriage. They are a strong-minded couple, fiercely independent, but devoted. It is a devotion built on strong mutual respect. My mother has now had to question that respect. Nothing like this has ever surfaced before. I'd be surprised if there were anything else like this. The circumstances seem to have been unique, and anyway I don't think my father is the type. I have tried to reassure my mother on these lines, but she is bruised. And she wonders. Bruised, but brave. She wants my father to pursue the truth, to find out what happened.

She wants him to accept whatever responsibility he discovers, that I can discover on his behalf.'

Esther looked at him for a moment.

'Your father has no responsibility whatever. The responsibility is all mine. I want you and your parents to be quite clear on that.'

Luke said nothing, and Esther gathered herself for departure. Luke took her down; and before seeing her into a taxi he handed her an envelope.

'My father asked me to give you this. It is a letter for you. He said I should speak to you first, and let you read this on your own. You may answer it if you wish; or just leave me to pass on the news you've just given me.'

On reaching home, Esther opened the letter.

Broad Oaks, Lynchets Wood, Dorset
19 May

Dear Esther,

My son Luke will give you this letter after he has spoken to you, and verified the news I have had of you. So there is no need for me to explain further why he has come. I had thought that I should come, but Luke persuaded me that he should make what might well be a strenuous and possibly fruitless undertaking. If you are reading this letter, then his journey has been worthwhile.

It is thirty-one years since you and I knew each other. If I have thought of you since then, it has been as a friend who belonged to a particular time and place, as many others that one meets and leaves in the course of a life spent travelling. Because of the special nature of our relationship, I felt unable to tell my wife about you.

It came as a very great shock to both of us to be confronted with the news, after all this time, that you had conceived a child by me. I can only imagine what motives you may have had in concealing this from me. But whatever views I may have on that, I know that you have given me nothing to reproach you for. It has been your decision.

Now that I do know – and I must accept the truth of it, despite the nature of the source (as Luke will explain) – I cannot just let the fact of my child's existence disappear again from my mind. I care very much about his or her life. This is why Luke has come, so that I may know what and how to think of this child, now presumably an adult. Perhaps there are also grandchildren I should know about, to add to the two that Luke has given us.

I believe you never met my wife, Thelma. She has declined to read this letter, but I have told her the gist of it. The matter is fully open between us. If you would like to reply in writing, I shall be glad to have news of you. Otherwise I shall rely on Luke to tell me what he has learnt from you. I do of course wish you well. I hope life has not been too difficult, especially if you had to bring up the child on your own. Now, I hope, you are able to enjoy the benefits of retirement.

I look forward to Luke's return.

Yours,

Harold Ingram

The next evening Luke went to Esther's house, and met his half-nephew John. At Esther's insistence, it had been agreed that she should tell her grandson no more than that Luke was a friend of a friend. Luke found her scruples old-fashioned, but was happy enough to accept this version for the time being. He talked to John, as one does to a boy of his age, about his school, his friends, the games and the music he liked. He asked him how he saw his future.

'Oh, I expect I'll go into a business of some sort. Perhaps have my own one day.'

'Here in Port Stephen?'

'Where else? It's OK here.'

John had the shyness and abruptness typical of boys his age, but Luke could read signs of character in the way he held himself. He was terse without being rude, and Luke noticed he did not grunt, like some English boys he had met of that age. He kept looking to his mother for reassurance in dealing with this unexplained person. But it struck Luke that he would one day be a man able to look after both himself and his grandmother.

The evening finished well enough. Luke and Esther had a few words on their own before he left.

'I have read your father's letter. It was a good letter, please thank him for it, but I am not sending a reply. I should like, if your mother will allow it, to give you a message for him. It is simply this. I hope he will not think ill of me. I have liked meeting you. Now our lives must return to their separate, uncommunicating ways. Please wish him well.'

'My father was prompted to write to you. But he said I was to tell you that I was his real message. My presence here would tell you that he thought of you, was concerned for you. I think he may want to write to you again, but he will consult my mother before doing that. You may be sure that anything you hear from him will be known to her.'

'Your father is fortunate to have such a good wife.'

'I think my father has always been fortunate.'

They parted as they had met, with a handshake.

He was able to bring forward his return flight and left on the next evening. Esther had told him his visit should not be prolonged on her account. He would have liked to spend time with his nephew, but did not want to press her for it. He remembered that he was not there on his own account, but as an envoy, and his job was to bring back news, good or bad, for his father and mother to consider. He sat now in the plane, putting that news into intelligible form for passing on.

Important as that primary purpose was, it was not what mainly occupied his mind as he travelled back to England. This trip to Africa had unsettled him. There was first the matter of his future. Being out in the big world again, even as a mere observer, he felt the smallness of how he had been living these past few months. A Dorset village was an ideal retreat, and Lynchets Wood had certainly been that. It was what he had needed. Now he felt the constriction of 'retreat', of withdrawal from the world. He was beginning to need something else. It was May already. He needed to find a new purpose in life. He had had ideas, and he ran through them once more. He had discussed possibilities with friends and contacts, in London and Oxford. Nothing quite came up to his expectations, though what these were he would have found hard to define. He was torn between an academic life, if that were possible, and a more active life in the sort of milieu that was familiar to him.

And there was something else. His affair with Penny had given him great pleasure; it had engaged his affections and his interests. She had been a wonderful companion, in bed and in all the other ways. She seemed to feel the same way about him. But it had reached the stage where either it developed or it faded. In what way could it develop, and into what? She was tied to Rupert. Luke had seen little of Rupert in these past weeks, and was unsure how he felt about his mistress's husband. He found it difficult to decide whether he felt, or even should feel, guilty. It was almost as though Penny came with Rupert's blessing. She seemed to have taken it upon herself to make Luke feel easy about their adultery. In so far as he had thought about the future of their affair, he had seen it as a gradual and mutually agreed mutation into platonic friendship.

Last night he had had a disturbing dream: the result, he guessed, of his meeting with Esther, his father's exotic mistress. He dreamt he was in Hong Kong, walking on the Peak. It was a brilliantly clear, sunny day, as it had been on that last Sunday when he walked there with Wendy. He was on his own, but he had lost someone that he was desperate to find. It was a woman, though in the dream he did not put a name to her. Far away, at the edge of the open space at the top, there was the figure of a woman, her back to him, walking rapidly away, as though escaping. He had woken, longing once again for the Chinese woman he had loved. He had had visions of her in dreams, since leaving Hong Kong. This was of a different order; it left him aching. He felt a presence hovering over every thought. He could not think of Penny without seeing Wendy, and when he thought of Wendy he saw no one else.

Rupert had arrived unexpectedly at *Coralita* in the middle of the morning. He had taken a taxi from the station. He was sitting now at the kitchen table, his head in his hands. Penny had turned from the sink, to listen to him.

'My friend is dying. Paul. He told me yesterday. It's too awful. They have given him four weeks. Four weeks! I spoke to him just a few days ago; he was the same as ever, bright, amusing, down-to-earth. He told me two marvellous jokes! And now he is face to face with death. He is on his own. He won't have anyone with him, just the nurse who comes in, and the doctor.'

'Oh, Rupert! How dreadful. What has he got?'

'Leukaemia. He told me he had been getting tired, too tired, but he'd put it down to work. We have been working on a project together. It's been a trying time. He finally decided to see his doctor, only to hear that it was too late, much too late. In four weeks, maybe sooner, he will be gone. He was offered treatment: they could have showered him with radiation, or pumped him with dreadful chemicals. But he said no. At best it might give a short respite, but at the cost of too much misery, too much pain and sickness. Paul gone! I can't bear to think of it. Such a lovely man! Such a wonderful man! I was getting to like him so much. We have been so well matched in business. We have had such fun together. The more I saw of him the better I got to know him. Now he and I have to put all that to one side; we have to agree how to wrap up the deal. There is a lot of money at stake. I hate money when it gets in the way of life, the little bit that's left. Death puts an end to so much.'

Penny did what she could to comfort her husband. He had come down from London, to unburden himself, to seek solace. After a quiet lunch he said he would get back, and left on the next train.

When Luke arrived home from the overnight flight, he showered, changed and rang his parents. Half an hour later he was sitting with them and beginning the account of his meeting with Esther. He was heard without interruption while he gave them the bare facts. He said little about Esther's appearance, what she wore, how she looked, how she had struck him as a woman. His father might want to hear him on that later. Harold concentrated his attention now on his unseen grandson. He wanted to know more about how he had grown up, what and whom he looked like, what his chances would be for scholastic success, what games he played, what his ambitions might be. Thelma was mostly silent.

The question of John recurred over the next several days, between Harold and Luke, and, increasingly, between Harold and Thelma. They came to an understanding that if anything were to be done, it should be to offer to help in the boy's education, in getting him started in life. But they would have to find out more about his wishes and abilities. Thelma did not contribute much to these musings, but seemed content to hear them being aired.

Some days later, Harold and Thelma were seated in the bay of their sitting room after lunch. Thelma was knitting while Harold, with deliberate signs of exasperation, was struggling to reassemble the pages of his newspaper into the correct order. Outside it was raining.

'Harold.'

'Yes, dear.'

'It is your birthday tomorrow.'

'God!'

'Well, you should thank Him. You will be seventy-seven. Seven years of extra time He has given you.'

'Is he being generous, do you suppose, or is he not in a hurry to see me?'

'He can see you perfectly well where you are.'

'That may be why he is content to leave me here.'

'I shall not argue with you. I know it will do no good. And I must practise tolerance and forbearance for your great day tomorrow. I wish us both to enjoy it.'

'Thelma, I shall be glad to have your support in enjoying my birthday. I find it too difficult on my own. Birthdays are a burden.'

With a triumphant grunt, Harold gathered up his newspaper into a readable form. Thelma ignored the provocation.

Harold continued, 'It is all so stupid. Every day of the year, every moment of every day, I am one year older than one year earlier. Why do we have to celebrate a number on the calendar?'

'There are times, Harold, when I think you take rationality too far. Now let me remind you, Leo and Margaret will be coming to see you at four o'clock. We have been lucky with our grandchildren. And now you have another one. I still don't know how to feel about that. I ought to see your responsibilities as mine also, but that is taking marital sharing beyond the normal limits.'

'You are an angel even to think of it. And don't imagine for a minute that I am unaware of it. You know, I have been trying to picture what young John is really like. Luke's description was very brief; but he sounds a bright youngster.'

Harold had made similar observations more than once since Luke's return. Thelma put her knitting down and looked at her husband.

'You would like to see him, wouldn't you? And you seem determined to help him in some way.'

'I must admit, I have been thinking along those lines, though without any clear idea as to exactly what I can do.'

'Then we must give some thought to what we can do, together.'

Harold got up and crossed to his wife. He embraced her. 'You really are more than I deserve. It is the only birthday present I want.'

'It may be all you get.'

Luke had collected Leo and Margaret from their school in St Giles, for a little 'tea party' on Harold's birthday. It was strictly family, and the five of them now sat round the dining room table, in the middle of which Thelma had just placed a large cake. 'Happy Birthday' had been written on the icing. Harold gave it a rather strained look. He turned to the children.

'I suppose you know how old I am today?'

'Yes, Grandpa,' said Leo, 'six score and seventeen years, which in your case is exactly twenty-eight thousand, one hundred and twenty-five days. That's allowing for the leap years you've had.'

'How long did it take to work that out?'

'It takes seconds on a spreadsheet. All days are counted from the first of January, nineteen-hundred, so you just subtract one day from the other.'

'You amaze me. When I was your age, I had to work out how long it would take to fill a bath with a leaking plug. That's much more practical. Plugs still leak. Margaret, do you perform these astonishing tricks of mathematics?'

'I am the numerate one,' Leo continued, 'Margaret is literary. She writes poetry.'

'Leo! I can speak for myself,' Margaret said, but did not do so. She had coloured.

'Every young woman of your age should be writing poetry,' her grandfather told her, 'it is the age to do it. And even if you find you can't, the effort is worthwhile. Didn't you once write poetry, Thelma?'

'Indeed.' She smiled at Margaret. 'I stopped when I met your grandfather. I found I had to concentrate on more practical matters.'

'Ah! And I started to write poetry when I met your grandmother. I was moved to do so, by being blind to the practical matters. That is the difference between men and women.'

'But we should not attach gender to poetry and spreadsheets,' said Luke, looking at his children.

Harold turned to the two young ones and said, 'Now, I have something to tell you; something that you should know.' He sat back with his right arm stretched out on the table, and spoke with his eyes on theirs. 'I found recently, and quite by chance, that I had fathered another child, thirty-one years ago. It happened when I was in Africa. A junior colleague of that time turned up here in the village, recently, and sprung it on me. Your father has flown out there to find the lady concerned, to see if it was true. That was the so-called "business trip" he made to Port Stephen. It was true. I had had a daughter, Hannah. She died giving birth to a son, John. John is now fourteen; his grandmother, Esther, has brought him up. Esther is a Persian-Lebanese single-grandparent, and John is your half-cousin.'

Leo and Margaret were silent. They had stripped their faces of expression, and were waiting for a cue from father or grandmother. Thelma provided it. She said, in an even voice, 'I was surprised, as you may imagine, and quite upset to hear about it. I considered divorce, as every woman should in such circumstances, but decided against it. The grounds are distant, and I thought it better to exploit the advantage it gives me over Harold.'

Harold looked at her, and smiled broadly. 'You never needed grounds for doing what comes naturally,' he said.

Luke laughed loudly, and the children, with obvious relief, joined in. Curiosity could now be unbounded, and they talked with much excitement of the newly discovered family member.

Margaret, whose turn it was to sit next to her father as he drove them back to school, asked him: 'Were you surprised when you found out about Grandpa?'

'Yes and no. These things happen; but it had never occurred to me it might have happened to my father.'

There was a silent moment while the three of them considered the application of this to the next generation.

'I assure you, you have no half-sibling hidden in Hong Kong.'

'Grandpa would have said the same, until someone told him,' said Leo, from the backseat.

'It would be different for us,' said Margaret, 'we have no mother. Daddy, we've often thought you should marry again. Of course, we'd have to approve her, first.'

Luke laughed. 'I'm not sure what your taste is in stepmothers.'

Leo told him: 'You could look for someone like Penny. Of course, you can't marry her, but someone like her. She's good fun.'

'She is,' said Luke. 'Yes, you must keep your eyes open for me.'

Rupert was home for the weekend. There were guests in the house and Penny was busy. They had to wait until there was time to sit down for a late Saturday lunch.

'I saw Paul the other day,' he said. 'He looked awful. He had a haunted look. He was trying to put a brave face on it, but whenever he tried for humour, it was like a skeleton grinning. I was trying to be normal. I couldn't bring myself to ask him how much longer he thought he had. I couldn't tell him how much I shall miss him. I couldn't tell him what I had come to feel for him since we started together. I couldn't tell him anything that really mattered. Anyway, his lawyer was there. We had to get through the business. I must say I do wonder how Paul could have chosen a man like that to act for him, but he is the man I shall have to deal with when Paul is gone. Poor fellow! I expect his judgement was going when he signed up with Colin Pratt-hyphen-bloody-Henderson. A real smoothie if ever I saw one.'

SUMMER

'Harold, have you given further thought to your new grandson?'

'I have, Thelma. I have just now telephoned the headmaster at St Giles. You were right: they do have a special scheme for children from overseas. I shall see him tomorrow morning.'

'You will ask him about scholarships?'

'Of course.'

'It will be difficult for us to find the fees without a scholarship.'

'One thing at a time, Thelma.'

'What did he say?'

'There could be a place for John, if he wants it, and provided he gets a good report from his present school; though as Hartley said, one has to read carefully between the lines for some of these school reports; but mainly he has to pass a written exam, which would be invigilated out there.'

'And a scholarship?'

'Yes, well, there are funds available, but he was not definite about the amount. It depends on what other deserving cases there are. And on how well the candidate performs in the exam. We shall have to see. I think any scholarship will have to be topped up. And I am fairly sure, from what Luke told us, that the boy's grandmother will not have much to fall back on.'

'Harold, the circumlocution is unnecessary. Esther is the name of the boy's grandmother, and if I am prepared to use it, I think you should.'

'As you say, Thelma. We shall call her Esther.'

>   Broad Oaks, Lynchets Wood, Dorset
>   2 June

Dear Esther,

Since Luke returned from his visit to you, I have been giving a lot of thought to what he told me. First I must say how saddened I was to hear of the loss of your and my daughter, Hannah, fourteen years ago. It is strange for me to write that sentence, having been given the news of her existence at the same time as news of her death. You had the grief of losing her, then. My grief is retrospective but still acute.

I have the impression, from what Luke tells me, that you have had a fulfilled life. I hope that is so. You seemed, when I knew you, to have a good future before you. And now you have a fine grandson, of whom you must be very proud. It sounds as though he will do well, whatever he chooses for himself, under your guidance. But, from what I read and hear, I can understand that the practicalities of life in your country may be difficult. It will be small comfort to be told that Port Stephen is in better shape than many other African capitals. You must at times be concerned that young John should get the best possible education and start in life, with good qualifications and with his intellectual horizons fully extended.

I have a suggestion. There is a very good school near here, in St Giles, which my other two grandchildren attend. It has a special scheme for children from overseas. I have spoken to the headmaster, who tells me there could be a place for John in September, if you are interested. Details are in the enclosed documents. John could come for a year, and if all parties wished it, he might be able to extend for a second year. There should be no great expense for you, since scholarship money is available, and my wife and I could see to his school holidays.

Esther, I cannot recommend this too highly. I should love to see my grandson, and to see him benefit from this opportunity. And please tell him if he does come, that he will have an old-fogy grandfather to keep an eye on him.

With my best wishes to you both,

Harold

'A wife would not normally expect to read a letter from her husband to a former mistress, but as you have insisted, I will offer a comment.'

'We agreed the contents. I thought you would want to see them expressed.'

'My comment is that if John comes, he should know that I shall be here to help his old-fogy grandfather.'

'He would quickly come to appreciate it.'

P O Box 4862
Port Stephen
15 June

Dear Harold,

I now have two letters to thank you for. I replied to the first through Luke, thinking it better he should bring my news to your home by word of mouth. Your second letter demands a written reply.

You are right that life in Port Stephen is not easy. Nor is it improving. John's school has for some time been suffering from shortages of staff and materials. He does well, considering, but I know he could do so much better in a good school. Your suggestion, I must tell you, arrived like a miraculous message of hope, the day after John had been told yet again that one of his teachers will be leaving. To come to the point: I have written to the headmaster at St Giles to say yes, in principle. I have spoken also to the Head at John's school here. He would do the necessary with a report and the invigilation of John's entrance exam. The only worry is the cost of it all. You mention scholarship money, but the brochure is vague. I'm afraid I could not find very much from my own resources, and there is no one in the family that I could turn to. I shall have to know more exactly what it will mean for me, and am asking for more information on this point.

I appreciate your good wishes and interest in my past life. It has been hard in many ways, as you may imagine, but I have nothing to be ashamed of. I had a wonderful daughter, and now I have a wonderful grandson. Naturally – and I am sure that is the right word – I recognise your part in all this. It was my chief regret that Hannah had no father: as Luke will have explained, that was my choice. I am very touched that you should now show such an active interest in Hannah's son, for whom you can have no responsibility.

I should tell you that I had not at first given John a full explanation of Luke's relationship to him and me. I have now done so, and told him about his grandfather in England. It has been exercising his imagination ever since. He joins me now in sending best wishes.

Esther

'Esther shows signs of good breeding, if that is not too old-fashioned a term.'

'I believe you would like her, though there seems scant possibility of your meeting her. I imagine she would send John on his own.'

'There is no reason other than money why she should not come, to see where he would be spending the coming year. And who knows? She and I may have a lot to talk about.'

'That goes without saying.'

'It would go without saying in your presence.'

'Ah! I see we have a new topic of conversation, in the topics that you will be preparing to discuss with Esther. What have I let myself in for?'

'You let yourself in for it all those years ago.'

Luke had invited her for an early supper at *Pant Cottage* and then to watch a film. She let herself in through the kitchen, and heard the sound of jazz piano music coming from the sitting room. As she entered, Luke smiled at her and waved her to a chair. They sat listening till it finished. He switched off with a remote control, and before he could get up she had crossed the room to sit on his lap. She kissed him.

'That was strange music.'

'That was Jimmy Yancey. He has a place in my pantheon. To pass him in the street you would have thought him a dustman or a janitor. At the piano he was unique: a limited range and technique, but within his limits he achieved perfection. If you ever get to heaven and hear the blues, it will be Yancey playing them.'

'I shall not want to wait that long.'

'His music is like making poetry by stripping out all the words you don't need, till you are left with the only thing worth saying.'

'And it's different every time you say it?'

'Yes, like it's different every time you fall in love.'

'You mustn't talk like that. And what's happened to the two-week rule? Surely, time's up?'

'It is more than two months since we first made love. We are well into extra time, and I am having to seek a special waiver.'

'I am the only person who can grant it. So you must behave yourself.'

'That will be difficult while you sit on my knee in this provocative way.'

An hour later they came downstairs and went to the kitchen to find food. Luke took a bottle of champagne from the refrigerator.

'We can start with this.'

'I'm hungry.' Penny wailed.

'Grab those olives. We'll eat later.'

When they were into their second glass, Penny asked him: 'You're renting this cottage for six months and it's already June. What happens in July? Shouldn't you be thinking of buying something? Most people seem to think the property ladder has to be mounted.'

'Most people forget that ladders sometimes have snakes at the top. But you are right, and I am always glad to have my decisions confirmed by a superior intelligence.' She threw an olive at him. 'The first thing I did when I came back to England was to buy a flat in London. In Marylebone. I have let it for six months, while I live here. It will be there if and when I want it. It would suit me very well, if I decide to live in London. I can walk to the Wigmore Hall. And from Marylebone station I can get a train to Oxford, to visit friends, et cetera.'

'I should not have presumed to offer you financial advice. I'm sure you've made a good investment. And I shall remember that you have etcetera to visit in Oxford.'

'You are incorrigibly inquisitive.'

'And you are shamefully secretive.'

'It goes without saying,' he began, but realised he should be silent.

'It appears to have done so,' she said, 'and it's a pity that its going without saying did not itself go unsaid.'

Later that night, after he had taken Penny home, he thought of the things that he had not told her. She was right. He was secretive. He had always been secretive. There was one thing he could never tell her, and one thing that he would soon have to. The untellable was his affair in Hong Kong. The thought of Wendy was still too painful to talk about. And as the pain eased, which of course it would, there would be less point in telling her. It was a matter of waiting until the affair had passed fully into history, had become merely one event among many, without significance. He wondered if that was how it would all turn out.

The thing he could and would want to tell her, at the right moment, was his hope for a job in Oxford. His old tutor had written to tell him about the new Institute of Asian Business Studies, recently established there with Chinese funding. It was extending its coverage; it was building contacts with the University of Hong Kong; it was recruiting new staff with theoretical knowledge and practical experience of Asian economies and money markets. Would Luke be interested? He was. He had made enquiries; he had spoken to the director, and had sent him the essays he had been working on since his return. He had agreed a date for interview. He would tell Penny about it next time he saw her. Or he might wait until he was offered a job – if he was.

Rupert sat there, ashen faced. He was home again for the weekend. It was his third sudden appearance at *Coralita* in as many weeks. He sat at the kitchen table and unburdened himself to Penny, speaking slowly, pausing between sentences.

'Penny. Paul is dead. I rang his home. The nurse answered; she told me he died last night: peacefully, she said. I don't believe it. He was in pain. I can't bear to think of it. He wanted so much from life. He had so much to give. And to have all that snatched away. He was my age, no more. We were such a good pair. We could have done so much. Now it is all finished. Oh, God! I must do what I can to keep our project going – if I can't find someone to take it over. I have no heart for it.'

Luke found Oxford busy but beautiful in the June sunshine. It felt good to be back. He had come by train, left his overnight bag at his hotel, and then walked to the Institute. There was a programme of interviews planned for the day, each one with an individual fellow, starting and concluding with the director. The interviews, which in fact were more like conversations, were in the fellows' offices, allowing each of them to discuss with Luke the details of their particular fields of work. They would feed their impressions back to the director, giving their assessment of Luke's potential, after he had gone to his next meeting. It was in between interviews, when he was walking down a corridor to the next one, that he turned a corner and almost collided with Wendy Chang.

'Wendy!' he managed to say.

'Luke! I heard you were coming.' She looked pale and withdrawn.

'What are you doing here?'

'I work here now. I came over last month.'

He found it difficult to assemble his thoughts, and was glad of the excuse to bring their encounter to a rapid end.

'Look, I have a meeting right now. I'm being interviewed for a job here. But perhaps you know. Can we talk later?'

He was flustered; she was distant. He looked anxiously at his watch. He named his hotel and they agreed a time.

She arrived at five past six. They sat in the cocktail lounge, the only ones there.

'You left Hong Kong very suddenly, without saying good-bye.'

'I had no choice about the suddenness. I was asked to leave at once. Because of you. I was told of another life you were leading; that my position, and the firm's, was compromised. I could see it from the company's point of view; and at a personal level I must say that I was deeply hurt. I could not bring myself to talk to you.'

'I thought it might be that.'

They sat looking at their drinks for a while, in silence.

'I will tell you,' she said, 'I did not like what I was asked to do. It was to help my father. You may remember meeting him once. He liked you. He had a big gambling debt he could not pay. He got into the hands of this horrible man, an ambitious politician, who offered to meet the debt himself in exchange for my services. I had to accept, for my father's sake. It was not too bad at first. My employer called it financial intelligence, and he thought my contacts as a journalist would be useful to him. But he came to demand more than that. I will not go into details. I did not like the man, but he liked me. It became unpleasant, but I saw no way out. You were one of the people I was told to cultivate.' She paused and looked at him. 'The others I mostly felt sorry for. With you I felt guilty, the more so as I got to know you.' She stopped.

Luke was silent for a while.

'And then what? What happened? What brought you here?'

'My father died. No, let me finish,' as he started to speak, 'he died just after you left. I could no longer help him. But I was released from any obligation to the man who'd been controlling me. I came to Oxford through a friend I have at the University in Hong Kong; she told me of their connection with the Institute here. I applied for a job and they offered me this one. I run the office that manages those connections. It is a good job. And you, Luke, will they offer you a job?'

'I have been hoping so. I finished this afternoon with Richard Morgan, after six long sessions with the individual fellows. Morgan told me it had gone well, and I would be on the short list. So I shall wait for their final word some time next month. I had no idea that academia could act so quickly.' He looked at her, searchingly, recognizing that if he were to take this job she would be a part of his new life; she would be, in some sense, a colleague. She had been sitting upright throughout their talk, moving only her eyes, from the table to his eyes and back again. He remembered this quality of stillness in her. At times it was a serenity he had found moving. Past feelings came back to him.

'I hope my presence here would not deter you,' she said.

'Wendy! I must confess I was taken aback, bumping into you like that. The director mentioned your presence here, at our winding-up session this afternoon. He had not told me when I saw him in the morning, hence my surprise. What you've told me does at least give some sort of explanation. If I were disinterested I would say merely that I did not want to judge you.'

They sat in silence, considering the unmentioned alternative.

Luke continued, 'If I come, we would be colleagues. But we have to recognize that the past is past. We would behave to each other as civilized people, with some common background that others would hear about. And we would have an uncommon shared experience, which we would have to put to one side. I am sure you are capable of that.'

He thought she flinched slightly, but she allowed him to move the conversation to other topics. She left to return home for her dinner. He was dining with his old tutor, which was why he was staying over for the night.

He slept badly. Images of Penny and Wendy chased each other through the night. Coming slowly to normality, over breakfast, he knew that something deep had moved in him. Penny was a lovely, warm, engaging woman. She had brought light and gaiety into his Dorset idyll. But she was Rupert's, and there would be no breaking that. And there was more. He had to recognize it. Penny was operetta. Wendy was the great, grand thing.

Solstice Saturday that year came three days after the actual solstice. So it was Midsummer's Day for the party. Compounding the magic and the madness, a full moon would shine upon the village from a clear sky, casting its midnight spell upon the vulnerable and the marriageable.

The day in Lynchets Wood got off to a good start. It was one of those sunny June days that attract the middle-aged and elderly to vigorous exercise, on the tennis courts, on their bicycles, or in their gardens – all in addition to the normal chores of shopping, housework, bill-paying and letter-writing. The younger elements of village society took a more relaxed view of what was appropriate. Many of them, after a late breakfast, wandered down to the village pub. When that closed for the afternoon, these young and healthy people – having no need for exercise – went home to watch the exercise of others on television. This activity comfortably filled the interval until the pub welcomed them back in the evening. The various groups of village society were thus ready, in their respective ways, for the great party of the year. By seven-thirty most of the tables in the village hall were filled, the few empty places being occupied over the next half-hour by the stragglers from the pub.

There was one special, empty place. It was at the first table on the left by the door, one that would be seen by everyone entering the hall. It was set with a wooden bowl and a spoon; there was a large sign behind the bowl saying: 'Please remember the Third World guest who could not come.'

The Parish Council had argued at length over the Empty Place. Some had seen it as 'token gesturing'; others had thought its seriousness a step too far on an evening of jollification. Michael Green and the 'green party' had won the day.

Tickets for the full complement of sixty places had been sold, so there were ten trestle tables of six each to be filled. Seating at the tables had not been left to chance. The female 'troika' had taken soundings, and had used their common sense, to place everyone at a table where they would form a congenial group. The three members of the Ingram family shared their table with the two Willoughbys and their teen-aged niece Alice. In placing Luke, the three ladies had not overtly considered his possible preference for sitting with Penny Hall. She was with her husband at another table. Conversation at Harold's table was not sparkling. Luke found it difficult to draw much out of the quiet Alice, and the doctor's wife, Esmeralda, seemed content to listen to her husband, who liked telling stories about past patients. Thelma tried to interest her in accounts of the places where she and Harold had lived overseas, but it was a struggle. Harold was tired, and not in a party mood; nor did he find Edward Willoughby congenial company. He wondered why his wife had placed them together.

Half an hour into dinner, Harold looked across the hall and noticed Hermione Bodleigh. Catching her eye, he waved. She was a woman he quite liked, a rather severe woman, very much of the old school, but none the worse for that. Thelma had said she would be there with her friend Ethel. But it was not Ethel sitting next to her. Harold froze. He saw the little moustache, attached to the unpleasant face of a short, stocky man. He turned quickly to Thelma.

'You didn't tell me Banfield would be here.'

'Is he? Where?'

'There, with Hermione.'

'Good heavens! He must have replaced Ethel. You know, I heard that Hermione had formed an attachment. I had no idea who it might be.'

The news did not improve Harold's mood. He turned his attention once more to the story of Dr Willoughby's that he had interrupted.

Elsewhere in the hall the lively hum of talk and laughter continued. At the end of the dessert course, there was the loud clinking of a glass, and composure of a sort began in preparation for listening to a speech.

All eyes turned to Michael, who was getting to his feet, and pulling various sheets of paper from his inside jacket pocket. He looked rather more untidy than usual; his beard seemed to have been tugged out of shape on one side. His smile shone more serenely than ever on his audience, which was coming slowly to a semblance of attention. Some of them were muttering, some were anxiously filling their glasses, others looked resigned. Jean, in muted mother-earth splendour, looked up at her partner with devotion.

Michael started to read his speech.

'Friends! And I think that's better than 'Ladies and Gentlemen', because I'm sure you don't want to be addressed as public conveniences.' There was a faint titter from a few guests. 'It is my great pleasure and privilege, as Chair of the Parish Council Summer Solstice Supper Party Committee, or the P.C.S.S.S.P.C., as some of you may know it better, to say a few words to you this evening.' He looked around the hall, as if to make sure they were still there. 'I must start by saying a hearty thank-you to the three stalwart ladies who prepared the way for this splendid evening's entertainment, which of course is not finished yet because there is more to come after dinner. Let us have a round of applause, then, for Dorothy Foster, Thelma Ingram, and my very own special helpmeet, Jean, and not forgetting Hermione Bodleigh, who helped out on one occasion.' He put his sheets of paper on the table, and started clapping; others joined in, either gladly or grudgingly. He picked up his papers again and resumed. 'Now, where was I? Ah, yes! It has been a good year for our Parish. We have secured an improvement from the District Council in the collection of rubbish, and we have persuaded them to provide us with adequate recycling facilities in the village. And not only does the village now have its own recycling facilities, it will soon have its own cycling facilities.' Michael's beam was ecstatic. 'You may have seen Jean and me on our recumbents. Well, we are opening a workshop in the village, where the old baker's used to be, where we shall be able to service and repair your cycles.' He paused. 'From bakers to bikers, you might say'. He paused again. The few titters and several groans were barely audible. 'And, and furthermore, in addition, we shall be able to demonstrate to you the advantages of reclining. My hope is that we shall persuade some of you to convert to recumbent reclining. Recline your way to health, will be our motto.'

He put the papers that he had been holding in his right hand onto the table, and waved the papers he held in his left hand. 'Now, where was I? Ah, yes! I must move on to the theme for our celebrations. As you know, Jean and I have always believed that we must leave this planet a cleaner and better place than we found it. So I would ask you all to help us by taking your plates, before the dancing starts, to the bins provided' – he pointed to four large black plastic dustbins lined up against the far wall – 'and scrape off your leftovers for recycling. I say this because after we have all finished eating, we shall move the tables to make space for a dance floor. You will see the table where the scraped plates can then be left, when they are left of their leftovers!' He looked up from his sheet and beamed again at his bemused audience. Two of the tables, where the younger people sat, were beginning to make sounds of insurrection. 'That will help to make our planet cleaner,' Michael continued, speaking more loudly; 'to make it also better we have again done the usual by adding ten per cent to the cost of your tickets to go to our special charity, Green Food for the Hungry of This World. And in case we forgot the pressing need to give to our less fortunate cousins on this planet, we thought it would be fitting and appropriate to set an extra place on a special table, a place for the Absent Guest, a place which of course is empty because the absent guest cannot be here.' There was a sound of bottles being picked up and banged down on tables. Cries of 'Gosh!' and 'Amazing!' came from the noisy tables, where they were now enjoying the evening more than anyone. Michael looked disapprovingly at the source of disturbance. 'The empty place is there to remind us that we must not forget that others in this world are going hungry.' He put the current sheet to one side and took hold of the next. 'To add to the entertainment, we have another innovation. It is the Green Barrel.' His beam became incandescent. 'It is not named after me.' There were hoots from the noisy tables, and cries of 'Why ever not?' Someone muttered, 'Why don't you jump into it?' The speaker persevered. 'The idea of the barrel is that you should all throw money into it, and then write down your guess as to how much money there will be at the end. The winner will get a five-pound gift token, kindly provided by the St Giles' Garden Centre. The money in the barrel will go towards the Lynchets Wood Biomass Project.' He put the sheet down and looked round. 'There! I think that covers everything.' And he sat down to rounds of tumultuous applause from a grateful audience. He studied his papers, and stood up again. 'No, my friends, I have overlooked some important information. I had not turned over this piece of paper.' He waved it at them. 'I should have told you that our innovatory Biomass Project was approved by the Parish Council at its last meeting. There was a very good discussion, followed by a unanimous, well almost unanimous, vote in favour. So we move forward, to pastures new, pastures green.' Michael's smile had now passed the merely ecstatic and entered the realms of the beatific.

There were shouts of 'Hurrah!' after which guests were able to resume normal conversation. Harold turned to Edward Willoughby and said, 'He should be given a hefty injection and put out in a field.'

'His heart is in the right place,' the good doctor replied.

'The right place for his heart would be as a transplant for someone who could make better use of it.'

'You are very hard on the man. His idea of the Empty Place is a noble one.'

'Noble? I have always felt that the proper place for charity is in the privacy of one's cheque book. I dislike these public displays of goodness.'

Esmeralda now spoke, 'Not everyone has a cheque book.'

Harold could only look bleakly back at her. Thelma intervened with a new topic.

There were two more speeches, mercifully short, after which the diners took their plates to the plastic dustbins for the dutiful ritual of scraping-to-recycle. The tables were then pulled to the sides of the hall, and a makeshift disco was set in motion for dancing. The choice of music had been another duty of the 'troika', and the compromise was agreed of starting with dance music from fifty years ago, working forward quite rapidly to the music of the present generation.

When the music started, Edward took Thelma onto the dance floor, leaving Harold with the sense that duty required him to offer the same service to Esmeralda. Luke, being left alone with Alice, had even less choice. On his second circuit of the foxtrot Harold was beginning to remember the steps, when he saw Hermione and her partner bearing down on him. He was spellbound with awed fascination. Eric Banfield was showing signs of heavy drinking, which Harold thought he must have started before his escorting of the disapproving Hermione. That severe lady was looking down her long nose with some disdain at the dancing partner who stumbled around her feet. He, being some inches shorter, was gazing up at her with intoxicated fervour. Harold had to steer Esmeralda out of their way, but not before his eyes had met his ex-colleague's.

'Harold!' Eric shouted. 'Great evening! Great!'

Hermione said, 'Eric! Do be careful!'

'Sorry, my dear, I must brush up on my dancing skills.'

Eric seemed more pleased with this mode of expression than was Hermione, but she was able to conceal her reaction. She noticed his general euphoria, which she ascribed to the pleasure he always showed in her company, reinforced this evening with alcohol. His euphoria would also explain his expansive greeting of Harold. She had found in Eric's personality a rubbery carapace, protecting him from the lasting damage that might result from slights or insults. Any shallow dent appearing in his well-being would soon bounce back leaving untouched his inner satisfaction, with life and with himself. She was aware of the shallowness, but aware also of its advantages.

The dancers moved on.

Shortly after this, Harold and Thelma were among the first to leave. On their way home, Harold made an unflattering comment on the Willoughbys, and said he thought he had seen the wife before, though not the husband.

'You have seen them both before. They were at our drinks party in February. You must have poured their drinks.'

'Oh. There must be something invisible about them. It would

explain a lot. He talks as though he is listening to himself in case there is no one else to do so; apart from his wife who listens to nothing else. And did you notice the antics of that awful Banfield? I wonder at Hermione. I always thought she was a sensible woman.'

'I think Hermione may be considering her future. She may see some advantage to herself in an attachment. She needs it. She retired too early, her pension is meagre and I believe she has lost some capital. Ethel's means are even more constrained. Their old age, when it comes, may not be comfortable.'

'It is a cruel world that treats the elderly in such a way,' Harold commented.

Back at the village hall, the elderly were leaving the floor to the younger ones. This being their first exercise of the day, their accumulated energies were released into dancing, to a sound that was turned up to full volume and could be heard across the village. It would cease at midnight on the dot, cut off by a timing device installed at the committee's insistence.

Hermione and her swain had the disco sounds as accompaniment to their conversation, in the front parlour of Hermione's cottage. On coming in, they had been given coffee by Ethel, who had waited up for them and was keen to hear news of the party. This was imparted briefly by Hermione, who at a certain stage gave her friend a look that could not be misinterpreted. Ethel said her goodnights to the two, and went upstairs.

Hermione had given some thought to this. After her inspired decision to take the unknown Eric to the station, on the occasion of his first visit to the village, she had weighed up his apparent attributes. She could see all too plainly his inferiority in moral and intellectual stature. She did not object to his lesser height, even taking pleasure in his upward gaze. And it was a positive bonus that he was weak and pliable. Above all, he had the essential attribute of resources. She had not had to probe him, on that journey to St Giles; he had been only too willing to tell her the size and price of property that he was hoping to purchase. Hermione had no difficulty in imagining herself as mistress of such a house. She had offered to keep her eyes open on his behalf. He had already paid a couple of brief but abortive visits, and they had established what might be termed relations. She found that he responded well to flattery. When Hermione saw another desirable house that was for sale, she took it upon herself to tell Eric that she could find no overnight accommodation for his visit, but he would be welcome to stay in the spare bedroom that Ethel and she could offer him. It was also the night of the village supper party, but she kept that from him until she had given Ethel the opportunity to think that it would be nice for her to offer their guest her ticket.

'Since you are viewing the house at ten o'clock tomorrow morning, I think breakfast at eight-thirty should be all right,' she said, to set the conversational topic. They were sitting on the sofa facing a fireplace in which a spray of dried flowers had been placed for the summer. The lighting had been arranged so as to show the interesting bone structure of her face, without revealing too many surface details. The hard grey in her hair was softened. In this light she might be described as handsome.

'Whatever you say, Hermione.' He put his hand on the seat cushion between them. She returned his look, waiting for the question she wanted. 'You will come with me, won't you? I do value your judgment, you know.'

'Do you, Eric? I should like to think I could help you. From what I have seen of the house, I think it should suit you very well. Though I'm bound to say, it does seem rather large for one person. Of course, I have been used to living in this little cottage with Ethel all these years. It gives one a different perspective, you know.'

'Oh, Hermione!' He took hold of her hand, a presumption that she permitted. 'I have been thinking and thinking and I cannot stop thinking about you and thinking how lonely I would be in any house unless I had you there to live with me.'

He came to a stop, trying to achieve a greater coherence.

'Eric, I'm not sure what you mean.'

'Hermione! Darling Hermione!' He was now on his knees before her, in the traditional posture of a man about to offer his all. 'Please marry me. Please, please!'

He had grabbed her hands. She gently but firmly released them.

'We have become close in recent weeks,' she conceded, 'but this proposal is very sudden. You surely know that you have taken me quite by surprise. Taken me by storm, I should say.'

With that remark, she smiled down at him, stoking his ardour to fever pitch.

'Hermione! Be mine! Forever and ever! I beg you!'

'Oh, Eric!' She put her hands on his shoulders, and smiling at him again, she said, 'Isn't it traditional to give the lady a kiss?'

Eric needed no further prompting. His ladylove accepted his passion with dignity and a show of tenderness. She made a mental note that excessive drinking gives a man unpleasant breath, but that there need be no further occasion when she would have to condone such excess. She diverted her mouth at a suitable moment, but allowed the fervent embrace to continue for a while longer. She then patted the seat beside her, bidding him to sit. She wished to talk.

'Before I can say yes to your very gracious offer, we ought to talk a little about ourselves. We are not youngsters. We have been living single lives for many years, each of us.' She gave him a questioning look. 'Eric?' she asked as though it had just occurred to her, 'you've not been married before, have you?'

'No. No. I've not ever found anyone before you. Never!'

'The single negative will suffice,' she said automatically and with an asperity that came from years attempting to teach the English language. 'Well, I'm glad. But you see what I mean, don't you? I have been here with Ethel for so long I can't remember. How could I leave her now? We are like sisters. And she needs me. It would be cruel to leave her on her own at this stage in her life. I could not do it.'

Eric contemplated a future with a second woman in his home.

'Couldn't she just live nearby? You could keep an eye on her. She could visit whenever she liked.'

Hermione had thought this through very carefully. She had seen an advantage in Ethel's presence as a third party in her married life.

'No, Eric. It would be too great a break for her. It just wouldn't do. I would always feel guilty at achieving my happiness at the cost of hers.'

The thought of Hermione's happiness, living with him, conquered all other thoughts.

'If we find a big enough house, there should be room for all of us,' he said with a final, fateful burst of generosity. 'Now, my dear sweet darling, say you really will be mine.'

'We shall be married just as soon as we can, Eric,' she told him, with an approximate date in mind. 'But listen. I think it would be kind to Ethel if I were to prepare the way. We must not overwhelm her too suddenly. Let me tell her of our engagement quietly, when she and I are alone, after you've gone back tomorrow. After we've seen the house and I've put you on your train. So when you come down to breakfast in the morning, we'll not say a word. All right?'

'Just as you say, my love.'

They embraced again, as the sounds from the disco reached a tumultuous climax. There would be no tumultuous climax in the cottage that night. Hermione had strong views on the need to keep the privileges of marriage for those who had earned them.

The next morning passed as planned. Hermione took Eric to see the house in question. It proved to be unsuitable, as Hermione knew it would; but it had served its purpose. Having put Eric on his train for London, Hermione returned home.

'Ethel, there is something I have to tell you.'

Ethel was the opposite of Hermione in many ways. She was short, very slender, and soft-spoken. She had always been happy to let Hermione take the major domestic decisions, and she felt an abiding sense of gratitude that her friend, so much stronger than herself, should have offered her protection. They had lived together for many years, since meeting as fellow teachers elsewhere in the county. Both had taken early retirement, on reduced pensions, being tempted by the terms then available, and prompted by the desire to escape the mounting stresses of their profession. Their small house and their life in Lynchets Wood met their basic needs and provided them with sufficient comfort, though there was little that might be called luxury. Had they not bought when they did, they would not have been able to afford it now. As it was, their combined pensions were now barely sufficient to meet their daily needs, and their economic future had begun to worry them. Hermione's contribution to the common pot was rather larger than Ethel's, having retired from a more senior position. Neither of them referred to this imbalance, but by mutual agreement Hermione had chosen the larger bedroom, and neither of them had concerned herself over the relative importance of Hermione's larger contribution and her larger personality. She accepted her responsibility as leader and protector. She and Ethel were good friends, sharing interests in art history and patchwork quilts.

Ethel sat now, facing Hermione in their front room, waiting to be told the news.

'Eric has proposed marriage, and I have accepted.'

Ethel almost jumped in her seat. 'Hermione! Oh, my dear!'

Hermione saw her friend's agitation.

'Now you are not to worry, Ethel. I told him that I could never abandon you. We shall set up a nice little home for the three of us. And it need not be so little. Eric is a man of means, as I have been telling you. We still have to work things out, of course, but I'm sure we can come to a suitable arrangement between the three of us.'

'But I couldn't come and live with you after you've married. He wouldn't want that, surely? And I'm not sure it would be the right thing for me.'

'I think it would be exactly the right thing for you. You would have your independence, as you have here, but you would now have proper security. If you were to stay here on your own, I don't know how you would manage. In fact you couldn't stay here. You would have to find somewhere smaller.'

They continued for some time to talk the thing through. Ethel was reluctant, and worried. Hermione was persuasive. Ethel began to accept that Hermione was keen to have her friend as a partner in her marriage to Eric. It would certainly be one answer to their common problem.

Harold put down the letter he had been reading. He and Thelma were at the breakfast table.

'This is from Hartley, about a scholarship for John. The boy did well at his exam, he says, and by good luck there are funds available, coming from a cancellation. So John can have the full amount. That still leaves a tidy sum to be found, but this seems as good as we could have hoped for. Read it, my dear.'

Thelma read. 'Yes, there is still a tidy sum, as you say, remaining to be found. We don't know, do we, how much Esther could afford?'

'We only know what she said in her letter, that it would be difficult for her to find enough. I think, you know, that if she pays the airfare and gives the boy pocket money, that's going to be about all one can expect.'

'Then this is the sum that we shall have to find. How is it to be done?'

'The only big item in our current expenditure is the annual holiday. We could cut out the fortnight in a Scottish hotel, and take the car to France. It's time we went back there anyway. And the only capital expenditure coming up is the car replacement. Well, we can keep our old crate on the road another year. We don't use it much. The other thing, of course, if we don't want to cut back on things, is to find the fees out of capital. What that means is reducing the amount we pass on to Luke. There's also what one or other of us might need if we get seriously crotchety. But Thelma, this is your money as much as mine, and it is a lot to spend on my side of the account.'

'We are committed, Harold. But I think we can manage, on the lines you suggest, and without plundering our capital too much. To be realistic, Luke's existing resources, if he doesn't fritter them away, which is unlikely, will not be greatly affected by the odd few thousand less from us. Our house will be the larger part of his inheritance, anyway. What's more, we seem to have entertained the idea of having John here for a second year, if his first one is successful.'

Harold placed his hand on his wife's. They looked at each other in silence for a while.

'You had better write to Esther. She will be anxious.'

Broad Oaks, Lynchets Wood, Dorset
29 June

Dear Esther,

You should by now have heard from Dr Hartley that John did well in his exam, and has been awarded a full scholarship. This is wonderful news; you must give him our congratulations.

There is the question of fees and so on, which I know has concerned you. I explained to Hartley that I wanted to take the main responsibility for this side of things, and that he was to deal with me on the subject. Under the terms of the scholarship, candidates are required to board, and it is these boarding costs that are paid, in full, by the scholarship, leaving parent or guardian to pay the tuition fees.

I am sure you will want to make whatever contribution is within your means. There will be various items to find: school uniform, other clothing, and pocket money are the obvious things. Hartley tells me he has sent you the school's advice on these matters. Also, no small extra, there will be airfares. Now if you add all these together, and find they overstretch your resources, you must tell me. We can't have the lad fall at the last little ditch.

I will be frank and tell you that the cost to Thelma and myself is not insignificant. We are not rich, but we can manage it without great hardship. It is something we want to do, and I am lucky in having a wife who gives me so much support.

Please let me know if there is anything else that needs doing, and, nearer the time, the arrangements you will be making for John's arrival.

With best wishes,
Harold

P O Box 4862
Port Stephen
5 July

Dear Harold,
Your letter made me feel that an undeserved blessing had fallen on me. As a grandparent yourself, you will understand the nature of my gratitude for what you are doing for my (and your) grandson. I was grateful for your suggestions as to how I might contribute. I shall of course want to do all I can. Being as frank as you, I can tell you it will be tight; but I can manage the extras you mentioned. I must also find a second airfare. John is clearly worried at the thought of taking himself to his new school in England. He has never been out of the country. I think I shall have to accompany him and hand him over to Dr Hartley in person.

My visit to St Giles will raise the question of our meeting. Of course, I should like to thank you and your wife in person, but will understand if you think otherwise.

Best wishes,
Esther

Broad Oaks, Lynchets Wood, Dorset
12 July

Dear Esther,

Harold has told me that you might bring John to St Giles in September. I thought I should write to say that I hope you do, and that we shall expect you to bring John to meet us all in my house.

People tell me I am forthright and sometimes intimidating. I don't believe it. But as they say in this country, you must take me as you find me. It seems likely that we shall find things in common. I am sure we shall have a lot to talk about, and I look forward to meeting you.

Yours sincerely,
Thelma Ingram

Rupert sat trembling, his hands on the table, staring in front of him. He was home again seeking solace from Penny. He must tell her what he had heard from Paul's lawyer.

'Penny, I don't know how I'm going to tell you. Paul was a crook. The man I almost loved, that bosom friend, was a crook. He stole my money. He deliberately deceived me. He had a lover I knew nothing about, a crack addict, a man with nothing who took everything. He took Paul, he took Paul's money, and then he took my money. You could say Paul was also an addict. He was addicted to that horrible, evil little man who had lost his own soul and then lost anything and everything he could get his hands on just to feed his stupid, infantile habit. And Paul was so tied to the wretched man, that he had to bankroll him. He was willing to become a criminal to feed his lover with crack. He was willing to do the dirty on me, to betray me. And he could do it with such bland assurance, such panache, that I was totally unaware of it. I just don't understand. I cannot comprehend how he could have done this to me.'

Penny came across to him. She knelt down on the floor, and put her arms round him. She was silent for a while. She hugged and rocked him, gently, like a baby. She cooed and murmured into his ear. And then she asked him: 'Have we lost a lot of money?'

'We have lost much, much too much.'

'What must we do?'

'I am hoping that the London flat will pay it off. I am not sure. Penny, my pet, we must talk seriously about our future. I am not sure I can do it now. I don't want to scare you, and I don't know all the figures yet. All we can do for the moment is just put everything on hold.'

Penny felt a cold hand on her heart.

She had been seeing Luke less frequently during the past few weeks. Since his return from Africa, there had been a change in the rhythm of their meetings. He had been up to London and Oxford several times. Often when she rang him he told her he was working on what he called his Hong Kong essays. She of course had been getting busier with her bed and breakfast business, now that the summer season was in full swing. And Rupert had been making his sudden visits, telling her of the fateful stages of the drama with Paul. That evening at Luke's when she had chided him with being secretive, she had herself concealed from him the story of Paul and its potential effects on her own future. She did not feel ready to tell her lover about something so intimate to her husband. She thought of what Rupert might or might not want others to know at this stage. The final bombshell that now ticked under *Coralita* had not come to light until after her last visit to Luke, and after the village's summer party. The Halls and Ingrams had exchanged no more than a few customary words on that occasion, before going to their respective tables. Contact with Luke had been sporadic, and mostly by telephone. She was coming to a view of him as an impersistent lover. He was wonderful when they were together, but seemed not much put out when apart. It had started otherwise, she thought. She had felt the need to rein in his ardour before it ran away with him and took her with it. She was happy to accept his lovemaking; it was not the first affair in her married life, though it was one of the better ones. But she knew where her underlying loyalty lay, and she knew that this thing with Luke could only be temporary. She was fond of Thelma and Harold, and they were neighbours. She did not want a messy affair with their son ending in acrimony. It must be managed. Luke must be managed. It should not be too difficult; he was a decent man. They could wind it all up in a sensible way, when the time came.

This was how she had seen it, at the beginning. Then events had intervened. The most important of these was the unhappiness of Rupert. His personal tragedy could have serious consequences for her, in the ownership of her little business and the whole wonderful thing of life in this corner of Dorset. She worried a great deal about her future, but it was a background worry. Right in the foreground was her concern for Rupert. She had never seen him so unhappy and she could not bear it. His feeling of personal betrayal had undermined his confidence and self-respect in a way she had not seen before or had to imagine. She felt deeply for him. She felt she should spend more time with him; but it was not practical to close down her business and leave for London. He, of course, had to stay there to sort out his problems, and there was little she could do to help in that. But he phoned every night, which had not been his normal custom, and always asked her to phone him back when she was tied up with guests. He needed constant comfort from her. It was all this that was at the front of her mind, and the great worry of it should have been enough to push to one side, to put into a little cupboard, the lesser diversion of this affair with a temporary lover. That was the problem, the big problem. She was worried, terribly worried, about her husband. But she was also worried that she could not give him the undivided attention of her heart. Luke had his own casual but compelling hand on that vital organ.

Luke had come to tell Penny about his prospects at Oxford. He had not yet mentioned to her that he had been interviewed for a job and was hoping for an offer. Now he had received it, just the day before, and he was overjoyed. Telling her all about it would be the easy bit. He had then to tell her about Wendy. He did not absolutely have to do that. He had no commitment to Wendy, and had no reason to think that Wendy would want their affair to resume. He was not even certain that that was what he wanted. It was not a matter of how the future might turn out. The matter was that Wendy now totally dominated his mind. Penny had been demoted in his imagination; displaced. The fun and the sparkle, the carnal joy, the light, easy exchange of body and wit, had had their day. He knew these pleasures were there for the taking. He had felt, even, that Penny had become more eager to offer them. He hoped this was not so. It was not virtue that pulled him back. He could remember women he had known casually in the past. There were women he had strung along after the cooling of his ardour, prolonging the affair, from laziness or moral cowardice, merely to delay that distressing final scene. It was often the line of least resistance to continue the diminished pleasures while they remained on offer. What was different this time was his awareness that to continue with Penny as before would no longer come naturally. It would demand a level of acting he felt to be beyond him.

He had not worked out what exactly he would say. He would start with the news of Oxford. He could then tell her of his surprise at finding himself face-to-face with a friend from Hong Kong: a woman he had known there. And he would leave it to the moment to find the words for the story to come out.

He was sitting now across the table in Penny's kitchen, and the first thing he noticed was her worried look. He played for time.

'We've not sat here before. It's your refuge from guests, isn't it?'

'I usually come to you, don't I? Yes, it's my refuge. Fortunately there aren't any guests this evening. Oh Luke, I was so glad you rang. We've not seen each other much lately. I have been very tied up with Rupert. There's something I just have to tell you. I'm worried sick.'

She told him the whole story, of Rupert's visits, what he had told her, how it had affected him and how concerned she was for him. Finally she told Luke how worried she was about her own future in *Coralita*.

Luke listened to all this, at first with a sense of displacement as of someone who has walked into the wrong theatre, and cannot understand what the characters on stage are talking about. But as the drama sank in, he experienced a strong and genuine sympathy for Rupert and Penny; and a feeling like relief that his own disclosure would on this occasion be impossible. Rupert's story could be the only subject of their talk. Luke's role was to ask all the questions that a practical, sympathetic person would ask. He set about exploring with Penny the details and the background of the case, the motives of the parties concerned, and the possible consequences. It was an appalling story, and he saw how hard his friend had taken it. He must comfort her.

They looked across the table at each other, their eyes locked in serious contemplation.

'Well, Luke,' she said with a sad smile, 'that's enough about me. What's your news? I saw Thelma the other day. She said you were in Oxford. She was definite about where you were, but vague about why. Perhaps you hadn't told her that you go there to visit et cetera?'

Luke was conscious of his glance falling rapidly to his hands that lay on the table in front of him, and immediately hoped it did not make him look as guilty as he felt. He looked up again quickly with a rueful smile.

'I have been offered a job. That is why I was there, and it is why I wanted to see you this evening, to tell you about it.'

'And you swore your parents to secrecy?'

'Not really,' he laughed. He was now talking slowly, spacing out the sentences. 'I just said I would not want to talk about it until it was settled. I have never liked people talking about my future before I know what my future is going to be.'

'Oh, Luke! Am I "people"?'

'Of course not, Penny. I'm sorry there wasn't a chance to discuss it with you before. We've both been tied up. But here I am now, hot from the press. I had a letter yesterday, offering me a three-year contract. I have a week to decide whether to accept.'

He told her about his interview, and the nature of the job.

'It sounds perfect for you.'

She looked strained, and the last remark came out on a forlorn note.

'Rupert's problems are going to occupy you for some time. You must not bother yourself with my business. I expect I shall say yes to the job. But I'm wondering what sort of help I can offer you.'

'Help? Just by being around a bit longer. Oxford seems such a long way away. How often will you come down to Dorset? Should I think of coming to Oxford? Do we meet in London? Or shouldn't I ask?'

Her voice had been getting quieter and quieter as she spoke. She was looking sadder and sadder. She reminded him of the waif in an old Italian film, *La Strada*, a young, helpless, too-willing girl with large eyes, not getting the affection she needed from the casual, demanding man she worked for. Luke came round the table, knelt down and embraced her. It was easiest just to hold her tight and mutter words of comfort in her ear. He held her like this while she cried. He held her until desire, like a tired old habit, stirred within him. He pulled gently away, kissed her cheek, and they said goodnight.

'It is worse than I thought.'

Rupert was home for the weekend. He told Penny they would

have to sell *Coralita*. 'I am taking a lodger in the flat. I must hold on to my base in London. I must stay there. I must keep at my work. At least my journalism will give me a more or less regular income. And I must pay off debts. Can you bear to think of coming back to live with me, in squalor?'

'Oh, Rupert! I'll do whatever must be done,' she murmured.

'A still, small voice. Poor Penny. All your hopes and dreams come crashing down, when the castle is barely finished.'

'We'll start again, one day, perhaps.'

'I have forgotten optimism.'

'I'll get the agent round in the morning.'

The display of blooms in the borders of Luke's garden showed what July could yield, even with no great effort from a gardener. It provided an unnoticed contrast to the sombre mood between Luke and Penny, as they sat in their usual places by the window in his small sitting-room.

'The worst has happened: Rupert is virtually bankrupt. We have to sell *Coralita*. It will be on the market next week; I spoke to the agent this morning.'

'What will happen to you?'

'I shall go back to London. I shall live with my husband again, as a good wife should.'

'Penny, this is so awful I can't take it in. Can Rupert not recover any of the money stolen from him? What is his lawyer doing? What are the police doing?'

'It's no good asking me. Rupert does not go in for details, at least not with me. All I know is, if there was a silver lining to this cloud, he would have told me. He hasn't, so there isn't.'

'Would he welcome my talking to him?'

'You could try. He was here yesterday but went back this morning. He will be cutting back on travel, now. He's busy getting a lodger into the flat, to help with the mortgage he has had to take out. And he will be waiting for me to join him, just as soon as I can finish up here. Perhaps we shall all meet up in London?'

Luke sighed, 'Yes.'

'Luke, do I sense that our affair is in decline?' She spoke sharply. Her face was pale, and she had sat up to look directly at him.

He paused, just long enough to steel himself for his reply.

'I had hoped we could wait to talk about that, till your other problems were sorted out. But it had to come up sooner or later. The fact is: we have no future, you and I. You must see that.'

'Affairs do not need a future. They are for the present. The present continues until it becomes boring, or until someone else turns up. Which is it, with you?'

'Penny, please. Must we take it this way? The last thing I want is to quarrel with you, especially now. It may sound hackneyed, but I value your friendship. I want that to continue. Can't we just wind down gracefully?'

'I am getting wound up. I want you to tell me. Do I now bore you? Or is there someone else? Or both?'

'You could never bore me. Let's leave it at that, shall we? Drop it!'

'Drop it? Just drop it? Just like that? I will not drop it. I want you to tell me. There's someone else, isn't there? There's a nice little bit of etcetera in Oxford, isn't there?'

'Oh, for God's sake!'

'When did you meet her?'

Luke was silent. He sat looking at the floor, conscious of the intense look she directed on him.

'I want an answer.'

'Very well, I will tell you. There was a woman I knew in Hong Kong. Our affair came to an abrupt end when I left. For me it was finished, completely. For her it had never really begun. So I started with a clean slate when I met you. But I have had to take stock again. I saw her in Oxford, at the Institute. It was totally unexpected. She works there now. It all came to the surface again, for me. It changes the way I feel about everything. There is nothing I can do about it.'

Penny was on her feet. She was even paler, trembling with rage. 'You hypocrite! You bastard! You played with me while nursing this secret little passion. You! Go to Oxford! Have your nice little fucks with your secret little woman. I'm finished with you.'

Luke was looking into the garden when he heard the front door slam.

The estate agent had come in from St Giles to show them round a desirable gentleman's residence, *The Anchorage*, in a much sought-after village near Lynchets Wood. He did not know either of them, but the office had asked him to meet a Mr Banfield at the house, so Mr Banfield must be the client. He gathered that the lady was not his wife, but most of the questions came from her, and he was careful to include the client in his replies.

'They are nice, big rooms,' said Eric, when they had completed the tour.

'Yes,' Hermione said, in a way that suggested the opposite.

'Would you like time to wander round again, on your own?' the agent asked them.

'Thank you,' Hermione replied. 'Eric, perhaps we should look upstairs again.' They went into a small back bedroom. 'This might do as the extra bathroom,' she said, doubtfully.

'Extra bathroom? What do you mean?'

'Eric, dear, we really shall need three bathrooms for the three of us. One for Ethel, one for you and one for me. It is so much more civilised than sharing.'

'I assumed that you and I would share. It's what most couples do.'

'We would share when we have visitors. Or Ethel could share hers, perhaps. But you and I ought to have our own little rooms before coming to bed.' She stroked his arm.

'It's not something I'd ever thought of.' He put his arm round her waist. 'What ideas you have! But what do you think of the house as a whole?'

Hermione noticed the twitching of his moustache, and thought, not for the first time, that she must find the right moment to suggest its removal.

'Well, it has its points, and I think we should keep it in mind while looking at others.'

'What others are there? We've seen a few properties now, and this must be about the best.'

'I have heard that *Coralita* is coming on the market. You stayed there, didn't you? You should know what it's like. What is it like?'

'*Coralita*? Good heavens! But that's enormous. And I bet it's more than I, we, can afford.'

For Hermione, it was an essential part of pre-marital discourse to establish the exact limits of what could be afforded.

She looked down her commanding nose. 'I think you owe it to yourself to consider *Coralita* as a house suitable for a man in your position.'

Eric found it difficult to contradict her assertion. They went downstairs and consulted the agent, who confirmed the availability and promised to send details.

Rupert heard the downstairs door shut, and footsteps climbing the stairs to his first-floor flat. He thought Penny had sounded a little distraught on the telephone the previous evening, telling him she wanted to spend a day or two in London. He went to open the door. She came in, in a rush, put her overnight bag on the floor, then turned round to face him with a wild stare as he closed the door behind him.

'Penny, Poppet, you look awful. What's happened?'

'Oh, Roopie!' She flung her arms round him, and as abruptly disengaged and hurried into the sitting-room. He followed and stood facing her. She came to hold him again, with her head on his shoulder, and stared unseeing at a corner of the room.

'Roopie, I've been so stupid!' It came out in bursts, interspersed with little sobs. 'I got myself tangled up – with Luke – he has another woman – he had one all the time – she wasn't there all the time – she was in Hong Kong – now she's here – she's in Oxford – where he's going to work – he must be in love with her – he must have been in love with her all the time – Roopie I've made such an awful fool of myself – I thought I was in control – I thought he was the one that was losing it – why should I care what happens to him? – I've got such a lovely husband – Luke's the one who should be suffering, not me – but I can't blame him – I hated him last night, but I can't blame him – I made an awful scene with him – he's really a nice man – I should never have let myself go at him, as I did – I should have had more sense.'

'Penny, Penny.' Rupert was patting her back and gently squeezing her against him. 'It will subside. These things get blown out of proportion, they blow up, and they fade away. There's no need to suffer over it. You'll get better very quickly.'

He pulled back, and said, 'What would you like to do right now?'

'I should like to lie in bed with you.'

'Goodie! Goodie!' he shouted, and rushed laughing into the bedroom pulling Penny behind. She followed with little laughs tripping over her sobs.

After the tumult, they lay peacefully in bed, holding hands.

'A re-consecration,' Rupert said.

'I expect people think we have a strange marriage,' said Penny.

'It is a strange marriage. That is what is so good about it. It lasts. Too many marriages don't last. Most couples expect too much of each other. Most people are selfish; they demand too much from the other person; they demand what most people cannot give: the chains of permanent enslavement.'

'We give each other freedom, but we accept a permanent attachment that binds us. It is a voluntary enslavement, but we have unlocked each other's chains. We trust each other. It is love that keeps us together, it is love that always brings us back from our separate wanderings. It deepens and strengthens, because freedom lets us see and appreciate each other more clearly.'

'Penny, what a great little philosopher you are.'

'Rupert, darling, what a great little lover you are.'

They came together again, lay in each other's arms, and slept the sleep of sweet relief.

Two days later, Rupert returned to the flat to tell Penny that all, after all, was not quite lost. He had taken on a new solicitor, an honest man, replacing the doubtful Pratt-Henderson. Rupert had just spent the morning with him. He talked about money that had been found, and the possibility that it could be paid over to Rupert in the not too distant future. And one or two of his own investments were turning out to be better than he'd expected. All in all, it looked as though *Coralita* might, just might, be safe. Penny should leave it on the market for the time being, and see what sort of price it could fetch from a serious viewer. But there was no need to leap at the first offer. Penny was so happy at this news that she returned to Dorset the next morning to discuss the prospects with the agent, and to enjoy living once more in the house she loved. She had also to contact several bed-and-breakfast customers that she had had to stall. She could resume at least some of her business for the remainder of the summer.

There was one thing that festered, one source of anxiety that left her uneasy. Her feelings about Luke were a mixture of anger, at herself as well as at him, and sadness. She did not know how to resolve the problem. It niggled, and she worried about the possibility of bumping into him in the village. She kept away from Thelma for the time being. When she heard, at the end of July, that Luke had gone on holiday with his children, she felt a respite. She had time to think how she might handle the problem.

July was a busy month for Luke. He accepted the job in Oxford, with a starting date of September 1st. He negotiated a month's extra lease on *Pant Cottage*, to give him and his children the use of it in August. His Marylebone flat also became free that month, giving him a more convenient base from which to house-hunt in Oxford. There was a lot to arrange, to plan, for himself and his children, while he licked his wounds after the showdown with Penny.

Then he took Leo and Margaret on holiday. They drove to Burgundy, where he had rented a house for two weeks. It had a pool and bicycles. They swam, cycled and played tennis. They had visitors, schoolfriends of his children. They read, relaxed, cooked and enjoyed the food and drink; they loved the green, undulating *paysage*. Luke, abandoning himself to leisure, achieved a measure of detachment from the problems of his life in England. He could look back with mixed but mostly calm feelings on his six-month interlude in Lynchets Wood. And he looked forward, again with feelings that were mixed and rather less calm, to his future life in Oxford. It would have its challenges: on the one hand, finding the proper academic rigour for his teaching and research; on the other, grappling with the emotional complication of Wendy's presence in both his professional and his inner life. The presence, now, of his children and their concerns helped to push his own to one side.

Margaret was a happy, outgoing girl, looking forward to her last year at school. Leo, his schooling finished, was more introspective; he had become more serious about life. With good A-level results behind him, he had accepted a place at Newcastle to read Engineering. He had come to feel a need to escape his background, to start a wholly new life, to explore new social and geographic horizons. There was something too cosy, too comfortable and constricting, too middle class and complacent, about the gentrified rural south. He might have gone to Oxford, but not with his father there, and anyway, neither there nor Cambridge could offer him what he had come to crave: the raw excitement, as he saw it, of a vigorous northern city.

This had all been talked through with his father, who had had to hide an initial disappointment. But Luke had come round to the idea, had come to accept that Leo's ambitions were the result of long, serious thought and genuine feeling. They talked, on their holiday, of Leo's future prowess as an engineer, being teased by Margaret, and gently encouraged by Luke. They came to terms with each other. As the holiday drew to a close, Luke felt more than ever how lucky he was with his children, and how unlucky they had been in a childhood without a mother.

The death of his wife all those years ago had numbed his emotional response to women. His liaisons, when they started again, had been superficial. Whenever he saw another man suffering the agonies of love, he had felt detached from any common brotherhood. He could feel sorry for the chap, but superior to that form of weakness. When he read or heard people talk of the conquest of love, what it conjured up for him was the notion of victor and victim. Conquest implied its opposite: defeat. He had liked to think of himself as beyond that sort of danger. And his huge success in making money had buttressed his detachment from mundane emotions. This is what he had thought.

What had happened to him? Had the slow attrition of time worn through his carapace? His affair with Wendy had been warmer, deeper, more interesting, more satisfying than any previous affair; but looking back on it, he could not recall thinking at the time: This is it, this is what I have spent my life waiting for, this is my one true soul-mate. No, of course not. I don't think that way now, he told himself, so how is it that the thought of Wendy has come to intrude itself behind everything I see and hear and think, as though it is she, looking out at the world from somewhere inside me? He could find no answer to the question, he could find no peace in thinking of her; there seemed no way to be rid of her.

Shortly after their return to *Pant Cottage*, Leo and Margaret took off on their own to visit friends. Luke got down to packing and preparing for the move to London.

One morning the telephone rang.

'Luke? This is Penny. Can I come and see you?'

She came in the afternoon. They sat by the window, as they had on that first afternoon, with the tea tray on the table between them. Luke could not tell whether Penny really looked different, or whether it was just his different way of feeling about her. She asked about his holiday; he asked about Rupert and the state of their problems.

'We've had a reprieve. Some of Rupert's money has been found in a hidden account that that crook was operating. It is not everything, but the serious pressure is off. And a past, rather doubtful deal of Rupert's has paid off. The result is we don't have to sell *Coralita*. We thought at first that we should keep it on the market, just in case, but now the way is clear. We are not rich, but we can hang on.'

'Penny, that's marvellous news. I'm very happy for you both.'

'Yes, it's an enormous relief. And Rupert doesn't have to have a lodger in his flat. He really was dreading that prospect. He is such a private and fastidious person. A suitable tenant, other than a very close friend, would have been difficult to find. Luke, here we are, making polite conversation, when what I wanted was to say sorry. After I stormed out on my last visit, I felt dreadful. I shouldn't have said what I did. I had no claims on you. You obviously have a long and buried past that I can be no part of. We ought to be friends. I'm fond of your parents, very fond, and I expect you'll be down here on family visits from time to time. We shall probably meet. We must be civilised.'

'Penny, you are very gracious, and it's more than I deserve, more than I had a right to expect. I can't tell you how glad I am to hear you say it all. We had a wonderful affair, didn't we? Now I can look back on it without that last evening spoiling the view of it. And I must accept my share of the blame. I am a secretive cuss. I should have been more open with you. It's just not in my nature, I'm afraid.'

'What is going to happen to you? Will you be getting married?'

'Good heavens no! Not yet, not at all, probably. I just don't know.'

Something about Luke's demeanour brought Penny to her feet. She looked down at him, 'Poor Luke. You're not very happy, are you?'

Luke stood up. They were close, but not touching. She searched his face, and she saw a small wistful smile as his eyes turned slowly to hers. As their bodies remembered each other, the space between them became charged.

'Don't forget I'm your sister,' she almost whispered, and he was conscious of her trembling.

She saw his eyes fall as he whispered back, 'One last time?'

It was as good as the first time.

As they lay at rest, she said, 'You are a wicked man; and without even trying. And I am a wicked woman. I came to make my peace, and I stayed to make love. I have committed incest once again, shamelessly, gloriously and with utter abandon. This is not what I meant to do.'

She had spoken with a singing cadence. He replied, slowly and softly.

'I could never have imagined this. But I'm glad it happened. It is a way of putting a seal on things. I shall now have a special way of remembering you, of remembering us. We have overcome. We have survived. Now we can be the best of friends. You are, as you always were, wholly Rupert's, but now you have no conflicting tie with me. And I, I don't know, but my future starts again, from a better place.'

'I shall feel a stake in your future; you must tell me how it unfolds. I shall want to see you happy. I want a happy little brother.'

'No more incest, little sister.'

'No more incest, dear Luke.'

Eric had come down from London to view *Coralita*, but was told on arrival it was now off the market. He was relieved. The three of them were now sitting in the front room of Hermione and Ethel's cottage.

'We should have another look at *The Anchorage*,' Eric said, thinking of the third bathroom that he might have to agree to. 'I have been talking to my agent in London. I can expect a price from my London house that should comfortably pay for this one, and leave a little bit over.'

This accorded with the assessment that Hermione had made of Eric's resources. And she too had come to see *The Anchorage* as the property that would best meet their needs and aspirations.

'We should need the 'little bit over',' Hermione said, 'There'll be that little bathroom to put in for Ethel' – Ethel stirred uncomfortably at this – 'and one or two other minor improvements. And I expect you'll want to have the house redecorated. It does look a bit shabby. I'll go and make us some coffee, while we all think about it.'

She got up and went into the kitchen. There was a moment's silence between Eric and Ethel.

'Eric, I've not had the chance to thank you properly for offering me a home. It is so kind of you, so generous. I don't know how to say this, but I didn't expect it. It's not what most couples do when they marry, bring along an extra partner,' she coloured at her own word, 'I mean a third party, as it were. I want you to know how much I appreciate it. And I only hope my modest little contribution to expenses will cover the extra that my presence there will cost. I understand that Hermione has talked with you about all that. I'm afraid I'm not very practical where money's concerned.'

Eric was trying not to look awkward while Ethel was speaking. He smiled at her.

'You're obviously an important part of the woman I'm going to marry. We've talked it all through, of course. I just hope you'll be happy with us. And she's told me what you'll both be contributing to our joint living expenses. We shall manage all right.'

Eric had an obscure sense, as he was speaking, of having stepped onto a higher moral plane than was customary for him.

'Ethel and I have been talking,' he said as Hermione came back with the coffee, 'We shall be a happy threesome in *The Anchorage*.'

Hermione gave him the softest, sweetest smile he had seen from her.

'I am glad. And I am sure of it.'

'I'll pour the coffee,' Ethel said.

'And we shall talk about our future,' said Hermione.

Eric sat back in his chair, and looked at the two women with an almost proprietorial air.

The next morning, Harold was on his way to the village shop, clutching the list that Thelma had given him. The July sunshine picked out in sharp relief the tight little terraces running along the hillside, making it again like a ribcage. He told himself once more how lucky he was to live under this reminder of ancient history, while enjoying the comforts of life in the late twentieth century. The thought of comforts reminded him, in turn, that he was clutching a list of some of them in his hand. He hastened to the shop.

On his way home, he saw Eric coming towards him.

'Eric, I hear news of you. But first, let me say I'm sorry we parted on bad terms that day you came to see me. I was greatly disturbed at the way I found out from you about my child in Port Stephen. Well, I expect you've heard all about it by now. Everyone else has. The daughter that I never knew died in childbirth. But I have a grandson. He is a great addition to my life, and if it were not for you I would never have known. So you are responsible for that. I must acknowledge that you did after all do me a good turn.'

'I'm very glad, Harold. I was upset at the time, myself, but I don't bear grudges. And yes, I expect you heard that I'm getting married. Hermione Bodleigh is doing me the great honour. And we are hoping to buy a house here.'

'Well, I wish you luck. You are certainly fortunate in your choice of a wife. Hermione is a fine woman.'

On his way home from the shop, Harold was still wondering what it was that was strange about Eric's appearance. He stopped as it came to him. 'Good God!' he told himself, 'That ghastly moustache has come off. There is hope for the man yet. She has started to civilise him.' And he hurried home to tell Thelma.

AUTUMN

Luke had not been in touch with Wendy since that one meeting in Oxford. There had been no obvious reason why he should contact her, other than to tell her he wanted to re-open their liaison. At one level that was what he immensely craved, but that was not a level he was ready to expose to her.

His rapprochement with Penny, given the form that it took, left him with a sense of imbalance, of disturbance, in his inner approach to the two women. It was, after all, not the obvious way to re-establish mere friendship with the one woman, while coming to terms with a greater, deeper passion for the other. He told himself to be worldly, cynical, more purely masculine about it. In his more lucid moments this seemed a sensible and helpful approach. But he was aware of a nagging doubt.

The day after he had moved into his Marylebone flat in early August, he took a train to Oxford for the day. He spoke to Richard Morgan, the Institute's director, to ask for time in meeting the requirement to live within the statutory commuting distance of the University, and to mull over with him suggestions of good neighbourhoods. They discussed the work he would be doing during his first term; and then he left to visit the estate agents who had been sending him details of flats and houses. He had not asked Morgan about Wendy, and he made no attempt to see her. He spent the rest of the day being driven to properties to view. He saw nothing he liked.

On the spur of the moment, lingering over tea in a café, he used his mobile to phone the Institute, and asked for Wendy Chang.

'Wendy, it's me, Luke. I'm in Oxford, house-hunting. Any chance of seeing you? Perhaps I could pick your brains about where to live. I'm taking the train back to London this evening, but I'm flexible about time. It's short notice, of course.'

There was a pause in her reply. Then she said, 'Can I call you back, in five minutes?' She rang back. 'I could see you at six, for half an hour. Would that be all right? Same place as before?'

It was agreed, and Luke was sitting at the same place in the hotel's cocktail lounge when Wendy came in at five minutes past six. There was just one other couple in the lounge, sitting at the bar in what looked like a romantic huddle. Luke ordered drinks. He tried to feel relaxed. He told her about his day in Oxford, his discussion with Morgan, the two houses and two flats he had seen, and what he thought of them. He asked her about her own apartment. They talked with only a slight constraint. When he mentioned an apartment block he had been shown into, she gave a perceptible start.

'You know it?'

'I live in the next block.'

He tried to read her face; he felt her unease. 'That would make us close neighbours,' he said, rather obviously. He wondered whether it had been sensible to ask for this meeting.

'Wendy, I feel a bigger distance between us. I'm sorry to have dragged you out this evening. Your heart is not in it.'

'Luke, I thought I had to come. I have something to tell you, something I think you ought to know because of what there was once between us. I have not expected anything from you, except that we shall soon be colleagues. But I want you to know that I have formed an attachment. We are seeing a lot of each other. It is Richard, Richard Morgan. I was with him when you rang. We were expecting to do something this evening so I had to discuss it with him first. Luke, it's quite serious, with Richard. Please wish me well.'

He looked across at the couple sitting by the bar. The man looked normal. Luke wondered if that man would ever know the feeling of cold steel twisting inside him. His partner didn't look the type to do it. He looked at Wendy. She didn't look the type either. He knew his face had gone white, and his voice was smaller when he spoke.

'Of course I wish you well. It was good of you to come this evening, in the circumstances.' He looked at his watch. 'I think we should drink up and go.' It was very abrupt, and Wendy regarded him with concern.

Five minutes later, not remembering much about how he got there, Luke was on the street, walking to the station.

He started his new job on September 1st. He had spent the preceding weeks concentrating on his subject, preparing work, reading and thinking about his future research. Thoughts of Wendy were pushed, with a great effort, into the background, from where they emitted a chronic, distant rumble. It was like a building site that would permanently alter his mental landscape. He felt a desperate need for other horizons.

Meeting Richard Morgan was the first hurdle for him on the morning he started. In the common room, where Richard took him to meet his new colleagues at coffee, there was general conversation that was easy enough. Wendy's name did not come up, and she herself was absent. As they were dispersing to their rooms, Luke took the bull by the horns.

'I must say hello to my old friend, Wendy.'

'I'll take you there.'

Richard left him at Wendy's door.

He knocked, entered and greeted Wendy in a crisp, friendly manner, shaking her hand across the desk.

'My first day at work. I have met my colleagues over coffee, but you were not there.'

She laughed. 'No. I am not academic staff. I am administrative. I find that Oxford carefully observes these distinctions.'

'I'm afraid that's true. Privileges are measured out quite precisely, in accordance with status.'

He declined the offer of a seat, preferring to lounge against the wall. They chatted casually, mostly of his efforts at house-hunting. He wanted to ask her how much she had told Richard, but felt this was not the time or place. Perhaps there never would be. He would have to leave it to Richard to bring up, should he want to. Well, it wouldn't have to matter. He left after five minutes, to start his new career.

For his Oxford home he soon found a suitable flat, within walking distance of the Institute. He would spend the working week there, and the weekends in London. He looked forward to developing a routine: he would enjoy his work, and work hard; he would keep his deeper disappointment to himself, and come to live with it. The woman who had come to assume such a vital occupation of his inner self would have to be found another, less intrusive lodging place. He must shuffle her into a small, dark attic room; and throw away the key. She must have no window from which to furnish him with her view of the world. Meanwhile the living presence in his place of work could be dealt with as an alien having only the outer shell of the woman who now occupied his attic.

He had decided to reduce his direct contact with Penny, after that last unexpected meeting. He would keep in touch with village affairs through his parents. But first, after just the one week in

Oxford, there was the big event of his nephew John's arrival in England, accompanied by Esther. Luke had offered to meet them at the airport, and bring them to St Giles.

The arrangements had been made; monies paid and committed. John was starting at St Giles School, in what he had learnt to call the Michaelmas term. The new international intake were to present themselves four days before the start of term, to give them time to settle in. The requirement of his scholarship to be a full-time boarder had been a source of anxiety for him. He was anyway fearful of arriving on his own, and Esther had accepted the need for her to be at hand during those first days. She would return to Port Stephen on the first day of term. Nor did she foresee the need to collect him the following year; after a year in England at boarding school, her grandson should have the self-confidence to return on his own.

There was, though, for her, the awkwardness of the inevitable meeting with her former lover and his wife. Despite Thelma's unexpected letter, extending the invitation to visit, Esther viewed such a meeting with trepidation. She imagined that it would be awkward for Harold too. She could not imagine how it would be played out.

'Harold, we must be sensible about this,' Thelma had said. 'We have been through it all several times; and I have written to Esther, as you know. If John is to come to our house, his grandmother must come with him. I am prepared to welcome them both.'

'I should prefer you to be present when I meet her again. And I believe you will be capable of liking each other.'

'If we can manage mutual respect, that will be a good start. We shall have to see how far it takes us. What she and I have in common does not, on the face of it, constitute obvious grounds for a lasting friendship.'

The day arrived when Luke drove down from Oxford to collect the visitors at Heathrow and take them down to Dorset. He took them to the bed-and-breakfast accommodation in St Giles that Thelma had found, where Esther was to stay; and he showed them where she should deliver John that afternoon. He had arranged to collect John from school the next morning, and he would bring them both to Lynchets Wood for lunch with his parents. Leo, not having departed yet for Newcastle, would be there also, with Margaret.

At ten past twelve the next morning, Harold opened the door to them, with a swift wide sweep, so that their first impression should be of him and Thelma standing together. He beamed at them.

'Esther, this is a great pleasure, and here is Thelma, my wife. And here is John, my grandson. Welcome, my boy, I can't tell you how pleased I am. Come in, all of you, come in.'

'Esther, I hope I may call you that, and I am Thelma,' she said, extending her hand. 'I have been looking forward to meeting you both,' and her hand was now on John's shoulder, 'what a day this is, to be extending one's family in this way.'

Esther smiled at John, as they stood in the hall, with Luke behind them.

'John, what a lovely welcome for us,' and then to Harold and Thelma, 'I think we are both a little speechless.'

'That is a good start,' Thelma said, 'you must get used to us at leisure. Now come into the sitting-room where Leo and Margaret are waiting for you.' These introductions being made, Thelma found a way of getting them all seated, before offering refreshment.

She took orders for homemade elderflower cordial, and disappeared into the kitchen.

'Now, John, you come and sit here,' his grandfather said, 'next to me, on the sofa. Luke, you and the children give your mother a hand, there's a good chap. We three will be catching up on a bit of history.' He chuckled at John, who gave him a shy smile and said, 'What shall I call you, Sir?'

'Well, not "Sir". Your cousins call me "Grandpa". Will that be all right?'

John nodded, and Harold turned to his ex-mistress.

'I recognised you instantly.'

'Age has preserved your likeness, too.'

'Age has done a lot of other things.'

'Of course. But here we have youth, with history all before him. That is what we must think of.'

'And that is why we are all here.'

Thelma and the others came in with the cordial, and conversation turned to the subject of aeroplanes and airports. At a look from Thelma, Harold – duly forewarned – went outside with the others to show John an English garden.

The two women sat facing each other in mutual appraisal, observing the features, the signs of age, the style of dress, the general manner and bearing; and each attempting to gauge the underlying quality of womanhood in the other. Thelma saw a woman whom she had to recognise as her equal, though of a different stamp. She could see that what must have attracted Harold thirty years ago was still potent. And she had to admire the composure, dignity and reticence in her visitor.

'A little obvious perhaps, but I told Harold to give me a moment on my own with you. It is important we have a chance to speak by ourselves. I was quite taken aback, you know, being told about the child.'

'You must have been; I do understand that. But it was unfortunate you should have had to hear of it at all, and quite unnecessary.'

'It was tragic that you should have lost your daughter.'

'Yes.'

Thelma waited at this one-word reply, then smiled at her and said, 'John seems a very nice boy.'

'He has been a wonderful companion. I shall miss him this coming year.'

'Esther, let me come to the point. You will want me to. I was devastated when I heard that Harold had had that affair with you; devastated, angry and hurt. The thought of that deception, lying hidden in our marriage all those years, deeply wounded me. I know men find it difficult to control their passions, but I thought my husband was different. I have had to come to terms with it.' She paused. 'And I have not known how to think of you. That is one reason why I wanted to meet you. You strike me as a serious woman, and I imagine you have always been so. But in thinking of what happened, what made me doubly angry was the thought of your using my husband – to put it crudely – as a stud.'

Esther started at this, flushed, and looked about to reply.

'No, please,' Thelma continued, 'there may be a more delicate way of putting it, but I wish to make the point. I try now to be objective. I try to understand your circumstances, as they have been explained to me, and I think I can understand. But I do not want to question you on the subject. I wish you to understand this: I have put that part of the past behind me. All I accept from it is my role as Harold's wife to help him in his responsibility as John's grandfather. You have entrusted him to our guardianship for the coming year, and we shall do our best by him. You may rely on me for that. You may rely on me to keep an eye on him, to let you know how he is getting on. Harold would not have the necessary feminine insights. I think, you know, that you and I would speak the same language on many subjects. I am sorry that we have so little time to get to know each other.'

With this, Thelma sat back in her chair, and smiled across at Esther, who was sitting up in hers, looking tense.

'It would be natural for you to reproach me more than you have. But I cannot, in all sincerity, apologise on behalf of the woman I was thirty years ago, for using your husband in the way you described. For one thing, he gave me a beautiful and loving daughter, and she then gave me my grandson. I would like you to understand that I had a genuine respect and affection for Harold, and I retain that in the memory I have of my daughter's father. I cannot honestly say that I would like history to have been different.'

Thelma stood up and crossed to Esther.

'I have had my say. You have had yours.' She bent down and kissed Esther with obvious sincerity.

'Let us be friends.'

'I should like that very much.'

A moment later the others came in from the garden, and the party prepared for lunch. They sat down as Thelma directed, and when John's turn came he turned to her and said, 'What shall I call you?'

'What do you call your grandmother?'

He looked at Esther and giggled. 'I call her "Granny Esther" or just "Granny".'

'Perhaps you should call me "Grandma Thelma", or just "Grandma", as your cousins do. Will that be all right?'

'I am calling him "Grandpa",' and he looked at Harold, who beamed back at him, 'so I had better call you "Grandma".'

'What a lot there is for a young man to take in,' Harold said, 'and what are you going to call my son, Luke? Has he told you to call him "Uncle"?'

John giggled as he looked at Luke.

Luke said, 'We have not thought of it, have we, John? How about calling me "Luke". It is the custom now. Leo and Margaret here may think you have the advantage of them, but that doesn't matter. It is the privilege of youth. Of course, it may seem strange to you, coming from Africa where everyone is more formal. You will find a lot of children here calling their parents by their first names.'

'We call our teachers by their first names,' Margaret told John, 'all except the Head. We call him "Head". Schools like to make their own customs, to be different. And new customs soon become hallowed. You'll soon learn it all. After a term you'll be swaggering around like Leo, lord of all he surveys.'

'Margaret,' Leo replied, 'you are as usual getting away from the point. I have been thinking it is time to have a new custom in naming our father.' The attention of the table focused on Luke, who might have sensed an imminent change in his status. 'Now the subject has come up,' Leo continued, 'this family gathering seems the right moment to make it public,' and he looked at his father, 'so why shouldn't we share with our new cousin the privilege of calling you "Luke"?'

Luke looked back at Leo, smiled at John and said, 'See what you have done? You have started a revolution. You have set my children free. Leo, Margaret,' and he turned to his children, 'we may as well recognise the total lack of respect that modern children have for their parents. I bow before this democratic assault. Ah, well, it was bound to come.' He raised his glass to them, 'Let us drink to your adult emancipation.'

Everyone joined in, with general amusement.

Luke turned to Harold and Thelma.

'I'm afraid I'm too old and set in my ways to adopt this modern habit. I must stick with "Ma" and "Pa".'

'Quite right, my boy,' Harold said, 'revolution is strictly for the younger classes.'

'I hope my grandson is not to become a revolutionary,' Esther said, 'it would not be a good preparation for his return to Port Stephen. But I will adopt the custom of the country, and propose that Leo and Margaret call me "Esther". Anything else would seem to be false. John, I hope, will continue for the time being to address me in the manner we are both used to. Changes should not all come at once. But I am already wondering if I shall recognise John on his return next year.'

'Don't worry, Esther,' said Leo, glad to use the familiar address to this impressive addition to their family, 'I shall see that he learns all the things he should, and none of the things he shouldn't.'

'Don't worry, Esther,' said Margaret, not to be outdone, 'I shall see that Leo makes the correct distinction.'

'There you are, Esther,' said Harold, 'John will find two pairs of hands, guiding him in opposite directions. It is the best possible introduction to the world of politics and diplomacy.'

Thelma asked John if he saw his future in that light, and the conversation continued in an amiable way until they dispersed from the table. Leo and Margaret took John for a walk, enabling them to talk without the hindrance of adults. The adults talked about the children, with the benefit of their absence; and then went for their walk when the children returned.

'We are taking it in turns to see this English village, through the eyes of our respective generations,' said Thelma, 'and this is how you can think of us, when you are back in Port Stephen.'

'I shall. It is lovely, and so different from what I'm used to.'

When Luke returned later that afternoon after taking his charges back to St Giles, he found his parents in quiet, reflective mood.

Later that evening, when Harold and Thelma were on her own, Thelma asked him, 'What was it like for you, seeing your old mistress after all these years?'

'I should prefer it if we could call her "Esther", as we have agreed. The fact is, I no longer think of her in those terms,' he said, wondering whether he was being completely honest. 'What was it like? I have nothing to compare it with. She has matured into an interesting woman, and I could see you found her so. But what you are really asking, what you want to know, is how do I feel about her now. It is difficult to say. What I had felt about her at the time was a mixture of admiration and companionship, and of course a physical attraction. The attraction faded in its effect, almost as soon as I left Port Stephen. The admiration remained as a memory, an infrequent memory, and overlaid with all the other memories that one has. I cannot say I have thought of Esther very often over the years. Until I have had to, recently. Of course, seeing her again brought it back. I will tell you a story, though I don't know how relevant it is. In London, some years ago, I went to a photographic exhibition. I forget the name of the photographer, but the pictures dated from the 'forties and 'fifties. There was one there of an actress, again I forget the name; I may never have heard of her. But the picture of her was unforgettable. She had been caught leaning back against a wall lit by the sun. She was wearing a tweed jacket and she had a light scarf around her neck. There was the sense of a cold day, in how she was standing. Her head was thrown back and she was looking straight at the camera. Her mouth was open just a little and she was smiling, with a slight surprise. She looked as if she had been caught just at the moment of falling in love. It awoke in me the memory of myself as a young man, the man I would have been at the time the picture was taken, some years before I met you. She would have been a few years older than me, but I felt that young man who had slept in me for so long had suddenly awakened, and if he had met that woman at that time he would have fallen for her with utter abandon. It was a strange feeling, coming out of that gallery, nursing somewhere in my bosom my younger self, his heart so strongly affected. You might call it infidelity in retrospect. But it was not the present me, looking at the photograph, who was falling in love; it was the buried younger me brought back to life, afflicted with those now distant pains of youth. The woman in question, if she is still alive, will be an old lady in her eighties. You must know: my idea of the ideal woman changed permanently when I met you.'

Thelma had been sitting quite still, looking at Harold while listening to this. After a moment she replied, 'I cannot imagine any such thing happening to me. Your story seems to show the ability of a man to allow one ideal to overlay another. It also shows the remarkable tenacity of an old ideal, as you call it, which properly belongs in a grave.'

'Then I am guilty of grave-digging. I am telling you of what belongs to the past. It cannot harm the present; it merely gives the present a new perspective. What we are dealing with now, though, is something rather unusual. Having accepted young John into our lives, we have also had to accept Esther. I say "we have had to", but I hope we can think of her as a person who has become a friend, not just because of her kinship with John, but also because of her intrinsic qualities as a woman. I saw that you got on well with her. I had hoped you would like her. I had hoped that I still would. Well I do, and I can like her without any of the other feelings I had at the time. The past is far enough away from my present self. You confront the past, then put it back and get on with the present.'

'Yes, Harold. I did like Esther. I do like her, I should say. She is a good woman, and I shall do my best by her. And you are a very lucky man.'

He came to kneel by her chair, and put his arms around her.

'I know just how lucky I am, and I never stop wondering at it.'

'Get up. You will hurt your hip kneeling like that.'

He kissed her, and got up.

'I shall get us a drink: a whisky and soda. We have earned it.'

The next morning, a Saturday, Thelma rang Esther to invite her and John to join her for the Sunday morning service at the village church. Thelma drove into St Giles to collect them, and the visitors had their first experience of Anglicanism in England, provided by the Reverend Tom Foster. Filing out after the service, they stopped at the door for Thelma to introduce her new 'family' to the rector.

'Tom, this is Mrs Esther Abou-Khalid, and John of the same name, who is Esther's and Harold's grandson.'

'I am delighted to meet you both, and so glad to see you all together.'

'It is a pity Harold would not come, even today,' Thelma said. 'Good gracious! Talk of the Devil!'

'Yes, but travelling strictly incognito,' said Harold, borrowing the expression from somewhere. 'I am here to make sure, as you make your introductions to the village, that I should be seen as an essential player.'

'Splendid!' said Tom. 'You take them round, Harold, and do the introductions. I will make your excuses to the Almighty.'

'Is He still accepting them?' Thelma asked, before walking off. She turned to her new friend, 'Esther, my husband is a godless man, as you may or may not remember. Fortunately, it is not a genetic defect. I am glad to see your grandson has been properly brought up.'

'John,' Harold said, 'always remember this: a gentleman never argues with a lady in public.'

They stopped to speak to the Willoughbys, to Hermione and Ethel, and others whom they knew among the church-going villagers, before walking back to the house for a family lunch.

THE FOLLOWING FEBRUARY

'Grandpa is proud of his new grandson,' said Leo.
'Grandpa is proud of Grandma,' said Margaret.

They were watching Thelma watching John, and Harold watching Thelma. Leo had come down from Newcastle for the weekend, to be at home for the annual 'At Home'. He had intersected with Margaret, performing her job with the canapés and helped this year by her new cousin. Leo had graduated to the dispensing of wine, periodic quantities of which found their way into the glass he had placed next to Harold's on the mantelpiece.

Thelma moved to the window where she saw that Rupert had become free. On her way she glanced across the room at Luke. She was worried about her son; he looked wan; there was a dark look behind the eyes; there was less lustre to him. Was he working too hard? Was there something else, a disturbance in his life? Harold too had noticed. Luke had come from London for the day, and there had been little opportunity to talk quietly with him. He was, as they knew, habitually reticent about his private life.

Rupert's smile, when Thelma joined him, cheered her up immediately.

'I notice three newcomers to your party this year, Thelma.'

She followed his gaze.

'Oh, Mrs Eric Banfield, as she now is, and her household. Yes, I thought we really ought to recognise them as such. I had to persuade Harold, but he has always had a soft spot for Hermione.'

'I can see she inspires admiration, but I am not sure about softness. I have always sensed an iron will there. Perhaps Harold feels they have a patrician nose in common, but his great thatch of dazzling white hair quite outshines her scholastic grey. Hermione is a great gossip, as you must know. I really ought to cultivate her more.'

'As a *ménage à trois*, they appear to get on remarkably well. Ethel is sweet, and I'm sure pulls more than her small weight. And it must help having a large enough house. Eric is one of the new class of fortunate property owners: he inherited an ordinary little house in London, which gave him more than enough to buy his anchorage in Dorset.'

They turned their gaze into the room, and Rupert remarked, 'I see my wife talking to your son, in just the same place as last year, when they first met. It is as though a year had not passed.'

'I expect their conversation reflects the passing of that year. It has been an eventful one for you and Penny. I'm so glad your problems are now behind you.'

'That is the wonderful thing about problems. The time comes when you can look back on them.'

'You are a great optimist. But for each of us there's a final problem of the one day we know will be coming, giving us no backward view – except in the next life. Do you notice any change in Harold?'

'Only that, in being a year older, he has slowed down a bit.'

'I am a year older. I am as brisk as ever.'

'Don't worry, Thelma. The problem you refer to will be a long time coming, and then it too will pass and become past.'

'That is the viewpoint I should be adopting. Now, duty calls.' And she left to circulate among her guests.

Against the far wall, Penny was questioning Luke on his work in Oxford.

'I have had my first article published.'

'What is it called?'

'"The Future of Chinese Futures".'

'I thought your interests were historical.'

'There is a small history of futures trading in China, but a much brighter and more interesting one.'

'And do you have a bright, interesting future?'

'I have a more than bright enough past to occupy my mind, and some parts of my past are very bright indeed.'

To Penny, the look that accompanied this suggestive remark seemed colder than it would once have been.

'The past becomes important when the future is empty.'

'Penny, I hope your future does not look empty.'

'You are avoiding my question.'

'I think I know your question. Wendy has married my boss.'

'Oh, Luke!' She paused. 'Did you have to go to the wedding?'

'I was invited, as a matter of form. And as a matter of form I found an excuse not to accept. It doesn't matter.'

'It will come to matter less. Plenty of fish, as they say.'

'I am not a great angler. To change the metaphor, I have reverted to pit stops. They provide a diversion, and are so much easier to manage. But tell me about yourself.'

'Well, I will tell you. A couple came for bed and breakfast, back in November. It was a heart-stopping moment. I fell madly in love.'

'It sounds messy. What about the man's wife, or partner?'

'It is she that I am talking about. He has now disappeared from the scene. Fortunately they were not married.'

'I'm glad I am not given to jealousy, but if I were I think I would be less disturbed by the choice you made.'

'Dear Luke!'

Nearby, Michael Green had buttonholed Dorothy Foster.

'I might be prepared to take the Church more seriously if I saw it being serious about our planet.'

Harold appeared with a bottle of wine in each hand, a red and a white.

'You are being too serious for a Sunday morning, you two. Let me persuade you to more wine, which I assure you comes from the great Gaia herself. I further assure you its quality is quite independent of the faith or lack of it of those who produced it.'

Dorothy took advantage of the occasion to move on, leaving Harold face to face with the angelic smile of his guest.

'Harold, I was admiring your broccoli when we came in. I said to Jean they look very healthy.'

'Last year's crop was a disaster: chewed to death by caterpillars. Some nutter told me I should wipe the underside of the leaves with a damp cloth, every day. Every day! I believe in attack, not appeasement. This year I sprayed well with herbicide.'

Michael's smile went into standby.

'I must give you some pamphlets on herbicides. I am sure you won't want to use them again.'

'My dear chap, I must ask my son to give you some pamphlets on time-management.' He filled Michael's glass, chuckled and pressed on, to dispense wine and good cheer elsewhere. He went up to the two Willoughbys, Edward and Esmeralda, who had just arrived. He remembered sharing a table with them at the village party last summer.

'Settling in all right?'

'We had just arrived in the village, when we came to your party last February,' the doctor replied.

'Of course, of course, I remember,' Harold said, remembering that Thelma had had to remind him.

'We are getting involved in village life,' said Esmeralda, 'I shall be one of the troika ladies this year, preparing for this summer's solstice party. I'm taking over from Thelma.'

'Splendid! Splendid! She needs a break. Does too much, you know. Now you two must circulate, mustn't stand here talking to each other. Ah, here comes Thelma to take you round.'

Harold turned round and found himself face to face with the man who had shed his moustache.

'Eric! Your glass! Now then, how are you finding *The Anchorage?*'

'Very comfortable, Harold, thank you. Of course, it helps having three bathrooms. One for each of us, you know. So much more civilised, I always say.'

'Really! Thelma and I manage with just the one between us. Then there's a small shower room for guests. Quite enough for us. Ah! I see your Ethel looking abandoned. Why don't you introduce her to Mrs Willoughby? Her name's Esmeralda.'

Harold gestured across the room, and went in the opposite direction. He was glad to see Luke with an empty glass.

'Now then, Penny. Are you still keeping this young fellow on the straight and narrow?'

'Still? He has always been quite beyond control, Harold.' She declined his offer of wine. 'I think the only control he responds to is what comes from his work. Did you know that Chinese futures have a bright future?'

'Being a historian, it has not come to my notice. Luke, what is all this? Does your dismal science allow for brightness?'

'Science cannot be dismal, Pa. Only scientists can be dismal, but that is a complaint easily cured by the pouring of wine.' He held up his glass and his father obliged.

Luke watched his father move to the mantelpiece, where he took the opportunity to recharge his own glass.

'My father looks less well. He is slower, more grey than I have seen him.'

'I was thinking the same. I hope nothing is wrong. Perhaps you should talk to your mother.'

The party continued in the way of such parties. Some guests did better than others: in whom they met, the gossip they heard, and the gossip and great thoughts they were able to pass on. Then they gathered themselves to leave, grateful to whichever couple it was who had started the general exodus. It was time for lunch. In the garden, snowdrops dimly glowed under a sky from which snow threatened to fall. Some of the guests wondered for how much longer the Ingrams would be giving their February party.

The unspecial guests have gone. Friends and family stand around the glass-fronted stove, which shows a glowing fire and radiates warmth. Outside, the sky is becoming darker.

Dorothy: They say we can expect snow. You had such a lovely day for your party last year, Thelma.

Thelma: It has been a full year. We have seen changes.

Harold: Some things never change. Michael Green still bangs on and bores with his eco-rot. He has only to open his mouth and cartloads of manure fall out. It's a pity his hot air cannot be put to better use. It could have kept the village warm this winter.

Tom: It is a pity that Harold cannot suffer fools gladly.

Rupert: Oh, Tom! what a terrible thing to say of someone. People who cannot suffer fools gladly are the most dreadful bores. That is not Harold at all. I believe Harold suffers Michael very gladly, as a perfect butt for mockery. Poor Michael, but he does serve his purpose.

Harold nods and smiles at Rupert.

Tom: I hope you are trying to be charitable, Rupert.

Rupert: Yes, Tom; you will be pleased to know that I am trying very hard. I must confess, though, that with some honourable exceptions, such as Dorothy and yourself, I find it very uncomfortable to stay long in the presence of goodness.

Penny: What does that say about your attitude to your wife? And all the other good people here, listening to such nonsense?

Rupert: They will know to make the distinction between their own, natural goodness, and the other sort that vents from a vacuous mind.

Harold: Well said, Rupert. I will add a further observation on the year that has passed. Hermione has shown us how successful an arranged marriage can be, when arranged by a sensible woman. And Eric is now a better man.

Tom: Last year we spoke of skeletons falling from cupboards. One fell, but had the miracle of being made flesh.

Rupert: The metaphor metamorphosed. We have been treated to a view of it.

They had not been looking at John, but did so as Tom spoke.

Tom: Well then, what about this young fellow here? John, tell us how you are getting on at school.

John looks uncomfortable at being singled out.

John: I am enjoying it, thank you.

Margaret: He is the object of great interest and admiration. It is a social asset to come from a country that most people know nothing of.

John: Most people have never heard of it.

Tom: Until you spread the good word.

John: Yes, sir.

Tom chuckles.

Dorothy: How is your grandmother, dear?

Thelma: We shall be speaking to her this afternoon. I promised to phone after lunch, so John will be speaking too. It is easy to keep in touch. Half the year we are in the same time zone. Yes, she is well, thank you.

Tom: Harold, we might say that you have helped to put Port Stephen back on the map, where it belongs.

Harold: Yes, no …

Luke: My father cannot help revealing a life in diplomacy.

Harold: As I was saying: Port Stephen is only off the map to those who don't look and listen. It has been having a difficult time in recent years. One thing it needs is educated citizens. Now, if we can wangle a second year for the lad at St Giles, his country's future will be assured. As for my other grandson, we must hope that Newcastle is able to educate its engineers in more than engineering.

Leo: Newcastle is giving me a wider outlook on life. That is the education I want.

Penny: And I am keeping Leo up to date with contemporary writers. Urban life has a literature of its own.

Luke: Any literature is better than none.

Leo: Yes, well, student life is pretty full, you know.

Margaret: I cannot wait to have that excuse.

Rupert: Now you young people, we are all breathlessly waiting to be stunned by the great achievements you will be showering upon the world. And all you need for that is to follow the good example of your father and grandparents.

Luke: Flattery gets no one anywhere, Rupert. I am immune to it, and my children are immune to exhortation.

Rupert: I totally disagree. Flattery gets you everywhere. I adore being flattered. I don't mind how false it is. I just lap it up and wait for more. Penny will tell you.

Penny: He's right. Our marriage survives on the flattery I dollop out.

Thelma: That is true of most marriages. The wife must constantly reassure her husband that he is the most perfect being in creation.

Harold: Harrumph! Every wife should consider her husband to be precisely that. And vice-versa, of course.

Thelma: 'Harrumph', as Harold says. It was always an important word in his vocabulary. Now I have caught the habit. It is a sure sign of ageing.

Rupert: I see no signs of ageing. I see King Harold the Acerbic, and his Queen, Thelma the Astringent, holding court in grand form, as ever, like genial Old Icelandic sovereigns.

Tom: Well said, Rupert, and we will not look an oxymoron in the mouth. It is the cue to take our leave.

Tom and Dorothy, Rupert and Penny, make their farewells. The family move to the kitchen for a lunch of soup, cheese and leftovers.

Thelma: I hope you will be here next year, John, or we shall have no cause to celebrate the half-term. Margaret will be away somewhere, either at university or in a foreign place for a gap-year. We shall rely on you for the excuse.

John: I really should like the extra year. It will set me up for the baccalaureate, back home.

Harold: We shall see, we shall see. You will have to persuade your grandmother, as well as the school bursary committee.
Luke: Would Esther consider coming to live in England? Just a thought. Of course, citizenship might be a problem.
Thelma: Well, it is not a matter to discuss on the phone. We shall be speaking in ten minutes. John, shall I go first?

Later in the afternoon, Luke rounds up the three young ones to take back to St Giles: Leo to the station, Margaret and John to the school. Taking his mother aside before he goes, he asks her to call him when she has a quiet moment on her own. She gives him a long look and asks, 'Are you all right, Luke, dear?' 'Yes, Ma, I'm all right.' Harold comes up and tells Luke, 'Don't make it too long till the next time.' Father and son look at each other, smile and shake hands.

Harold and Thelma stand in the doorway, watching their son and the three grandchildren depart. Darkness has come early. It has begun to snow. They stand for a moment longer, to watch the snow falling slow and silent. A street lamp at the end of the lane makes a flickering light through the falling white curtain.